He held her tight.

"Lighten up, O'Shea. It was a compliment. I like your hair down." He tilted his head to peer into her eyes as he rumbled his absurd comment. "The way you wore it last night."

Mere inches separated her face from his and her lips tightened in annoyance. Did he actually expect her to respond to that? Stick to the plan, Cara. Ignore him. She stared blankly over his shoulder.

"All those wild curls beg a man to sink his fingers in to see if they're as soft as they appear."

Her mouth twitched with the need to respond. Okay, maybe someone who'd spent his life being slammed to the ground by three-hundred-pound behemoths wasn't capable of reading the subtleties of body language. He probably had his brain scrambled so often he needed verbal cues to understand not all women appreciated his brand of juvenile machismo.

"You know, Finnegan," she spoke nonchalantly, staring straight ahead as though he didn't bother her at all. "There are medications that can help lessen the mental complications of brain damage from repeated concussions. Someone in the front office of the NFL should be able to give you the name of a doctor who can prescribe them."

He chuckled, and she made the mistake of shifting her eyes back to his. They twinkled with mirth above a bright, white smile. The riotous fluttering in her belly brought a slight rush of nausea. Dismayed to discover those damn butterflies weren't dead after all, she looked away.

Was brain damage contagious?

Cara O'Shea's Return

by

Mackenzie Crowne

Cara O'Shea's Return

COPYRIGHT © 2013 by Mackenzie Crowne

Cover Art by *Kim Mendoza*

The Wild Rose Press, Inc.
PO Box 708
Adams Basin, NY 14410-0708
Visit us at www.thewildrosepress.com

Publishing History
First Champagne Rose Edition, 2013
Print ISBN 978-1-62830-080-2
Digital ISBN 978-1-62830-059-8

Published in the United States of America

Dedication

For Leeta.
Because girlfriends are a gift from God.

Chapter One

"The caterers will be here in twenty minutes, Charles. Stop twitching."

Five-foot-six with thick black hair, sparkling hazel eyes, and a slim frame, Cara's assistant would have been called petite, and pretty, if not for the well-developed musculature he worked on seven days a week.

"Easy for you to say." He matched her long stride across the expanse of gleaming parquet flooring. "You're out of here tomorrow. I, on the other hand, am left to deal with the wrath of Evan Malone. He's not happy with you leaving."

"He understands why I am."

"Well, I wish someone would explain it to me. Podunk, Massachusetts." His shoulders quivered in a dainty shudder.

"Palmerton."

"Same thing."

"You're a frigging riot, *Chuck*. Didn't Evan tell you not to harass the talent?"

"Talent?" He followed her across the gallery's main room, a dubious frown on his face. He nodded his head in the direction of one of her oils, a bold splash of color and shape in the modern style. "A monkey could have painted that."

Cara laughed as she always did when he made the comment. "Yeah, I know, it's crap. Who knew I could splash a little paint on a canvas and get rich?"

His snicker was arrogant, but he sobered quickly. "What are you going to do in Palmerton? Palmerton, for heaven's sake, not even Boston!"

"I'm going home." A city creature down to his manicured nails, he'd never understand her desire to return to the small town where she grew up. "And to answer your question, I'm going to paint, of course, without the chaos of the city to distract me."

"You'll be stir crazy in a week." He shook his head.

"Aw, are you going to miss me, Charles?" She stopped and turned, wrapping her arms around him and hugging him close. "I always knew you had a little bit of a crush on me."

He pushed out of her embrace after returning it for several heartbeats. "A crush?" He glanced down his nose at her, which made her laugh considering he was half a foot shorter than she and had to look up to do it. "On a no-talent Amazon with a bad temper?" His snort was quick and concise. "You aren't my type, honey."

She grinned as they walked down the center of the atrium. To tell the truth, she supposed she'd miss New York, or more precisely, the gallery and the friends she had made here, but her self-imposed exile had gone on far too long. Her recent success allowed her to work anywhere, and she wanted to go home.

"The second bar goes here." She waved a narrow hand at the space outside the door to one of the lounges.

He nodded, making a notation on his list. "So, have you told your family you're moving back yet?"

She stiffened, then immediately rolled her shoulders in an effort to relax. Seeing her father again would be difficult, but she had no illusions she would be able to avoid him for long. In a town the size of Palmerton, they were bound to run into one another. Erin's wedding next week made the possibility of a meeting, sooner rather than later, inevitable.

"I told my sisters last week. Erin was thrilled I'll be back in time to be fitted for my bridesmaid dress and Shan promised to contact a Realtor friend to line up a few possible locations for my new studio."

"Now that you're a famous artist, Podunk will probably throw a parade to welcome back their most famous citizen."

She headed back toward her office, and he scurried to keep up with her long strides. "Actually, they've already done that."

"What?" He halted just inside her office door, wearing an affronted scowl at not having been informed of an event he would have crowed over. "They threw you a parade and you didn't tell us?"

"They threw a parade to welcome home the town's most famous citizen a couple of years ago. I missed it, so I can't give you any of the juicy details."

She slipped into the chair behind her desk, trying not to laugh at the disappointed frown on her assistant's face. She was going to miss Charles. The man gossiped like a fishwife, and hated when she didn't cooperate.

He propped a hip on the corner of her desk, swinging one leg casually. "You've been the talk of the art world since your first exhibit six months ago. Who from Podunk could be more famous than you?"

Finn the Fine.

The name she and her friend Meggy had given Palmerton's famous football hero when they were girls echoed in her head. She mentally shook the memory clear.

"Michael Finnegan."

Charles' face morphed from curiosity to incredulity.

"*The* Michael Finnegan?"

She grimaced.

"Fabulous Finn is from Podunk?"

"Palmerton."

"Whatever." He waved his hand dismissively. "Do you actually know him?" His eyes gleamed with interest and she saw a lengthy inquisition coming on.

"The caterers will be here in…" She checked her watch. "Ten minutes."

"Oh, please. You know I'll just keep at you until you tell me all there is to know about that delicious man."

"That's all there is to know." She slipped a stack of papers into the top drawer of her desk. "I don't know him. Not really. We just grew up in the same town."

"He's gorgeous." His smile grew wistful. He leaned toward her. "What's he like?"

She laughed. "He's not your type, Charles."

His wistful smile turned snide. "If you don't know him, how do you know he's not my type?"

An image of Finn, his laser blue eyes full of dark male awareness flashed through her mind, followed by the memory of his smiling face as he sat having dinner with a stunning blonde, who wasn't his wife.

Cara hadn't been the least bit surprised to read in the paper a month after that chance encounter, that Mrs.

Finnegan had filed for divorce. And following that article had come others, hundreds of others. A week didn't pass without a picture or an article detailing Finn's latest romantic conquest. The well-watched portico of his Beacon Hill penthouse had become famous through the photographs of the parade of young lovelies swinging through the revolving door of his exclusive address. Since his retirement from pro ball four years ago, his status as a stud had been splashed across the covers of both sports and entertainment publications on a regular basis.

When it came to women, Finn was as fickle as a kid in a candy store.

"Have you picked up a magazine lately?"

"You can't trust what's on those rags. They project an image, but rarely the truth."

Plucking a rose from the arrangement on the corner of her desk, she brushed its soft petals against the curve of her cheek.

"Take my word for it, Charles. I've seen your type and…" He raised his perfect eyebrows and waited. She did her best to shove the conversation in a different direction. "Come to think of it, yours looks a lot like mine."

The gambit worked.

"Honey, my type wouldn't give you a second look. And how would you even know what yours is when you never actually associate with men?"

The rose stilled against her cheek. "I associate with men all the time."

"That's business. Brushing off the hunks that are always hitting on you isn't the same as socializing."

An unladylike snort was her only response.

"When was the last time you had a date?"

"What are you, my mother?" It was an old argument. He'd been worrying about her love life, or lack thereof, since the day Evan hired him. "Maybe I just don't like men."

"Oh, you like men, honey. They just scare the crap out of you, and so far none of them have been brave enough to get close enough to change that. But mark my words." His wagging finger accompanied his prediction. "One of these days, some big, strong brute is going to ignore that no trespassing sign you wear on your sleeve and grab hold of that luscious body, and then you'll realize..."

"Showtime." Spotting Evan Malone walking through the front doors, she rose to her feet. Charles narrowed his eyes, but jumped from her desk to go meet the gallery owner.

She sighed, relieved she had managed to steer the conversation away from Michael Finnegan, and that Charles still hadn't picked up a single vibe from the one and only time she *had* put away that no trespassing sign.

She smiled across the studio's large foyer at the man who had become a friend as well as one time lover. Evan had been there to help her sort through the pieces of her shattered life. She knew he was disappointed in her decision to leave New York, but while his friendship meant the world to her, it was time to go home.

Chapter Two

Not much changed in Palmerton, Massachusetts. After eight years, the tiny suburb, north of Boston, maintained its small town feel. The town hall bustled with activity, the Blue Bell Diner continued as headquarters for the local gossip mill, and standing in front of Maive Cataldo's house still made Cara want to run like hell.

And yet, the cozy, craftsman style home didn't have the sinister aura she remembered from childhood. Brightly colored geraniums lined the brick walkway and a wooden swing hung from the branch of the scraggly old apple tree Cara once climbed on a dare.

She double checked the stenciled numbers beside the front door. One-fifty-one. She was at the right address, but couldn't picture the cantankerous Mrs. Cataldo whiling away a summer afternoon on a wood and rope swing.

Behind her, the soft purr of a well-tuned engine came to an abrupt halt. Cara shrugged the welcoming sentiment of the charming swing aside and turned to find Jill Carlson climbing from a sleek luxury vehicle.

Upon arriving in town, Cara had been surprised to learn Shan's best friend from high school was the town's only real estate agent. The slim blonde's love of gossip certainly hadn't changed. Jill talked Cara's ear off, filling her in on the current happenings in town, while dragging her from one potential property to another. But she couldn't fault Jill's professionalism. She was no happier dealing with Maive Cataldo than Cara, but hadn't wasted any time setting up a meeting once Cara made her choice.

"Ready to face the dragon lady?" Jill slipped the strap of a leather briefcase over one shoulder and stepped to the curb.

Cara smirked. "Suck it up, Carlson. This is important to me."

White teeth flashed in Jill's grin. They made their way up the walkway together to climb the three steps to the porch. Cara pressed her finger to the doorbell.

Jill fisted her free hand at her waist. "Damn, my palms are sweating."

Cara flicked her a fulminating glance just before the door opened and an ancient, white-haired woman dressed in a seersucker day-dress, straight out of the nineteen forties, stood glaring at them.

"Well, are you going to stand there all day?" The tiny sprite spun about and retreated down the hall. Cara and Jill exchanged a grimace before following the dragon lady into her lair.

She disappeared through a doorway. When Cara and Jill joined her in the formal parlor, she was lowering onto an antique settee Cara figured came into existence about the same time as Maive herself. Blooms the size of cabbages covered the walls, the linen wallpaper pristine despite its dated style, above elaborate wainscoting. The ten-foot high ceiling was a masterpiece of intricately carved panels.

Jill cleared her throat. "This is Cara O'Shea, Mrs.

Cataldo."

"I know who she is." Maive sniffed. "You called and interrupted my show to tell me she wanted to meet with me, didn't you?"

"Yes, I...well."

"Sit down, for heaven's sake. I'll get a crick in my neck looking up at the two of you."

Cara sat on a delicate wingback chair, while Jill scrambled to the couch across from the settee.

Maive studied Cara with a keen eye. "So, now that you're a famous artist, you've decided to come home?"

Surprised, Cara shifted in her chair. "You know about my work?"

"I can read, can't I? Your picture's been plastered in the Arts section of the Times for months." Her aged blue eyes sparkled with accusation. "I'm always interested in the doings of someone who has the audacity to steal apples from my tree."

Cara's years in Manhattan had thrown her up against Maive's kind before, and the trick was to show no fear. She crossed her legs and fought back a smile. "I didn't think you knew about that."

Maive harrumphed.

"I stole them on a dare." The smile won. "They were very good apples."

Maive pointed a spindly finger at her. "You're a sly one, Cara O'Shea. Got that from living in the big city all these years, no doubt. So, what is it you want?"

What did she want? She shot a questioning glance at Jill, who stared at the ceiling as if she expected three headed dogs to sprout from the panels.

"Don't look to her." Maive's scolding tone drew Cara's gaze. "She's afraid of her own shadow. You want something from me, you ask me yourself."

Okay, she could dance with the old biddy.

"I want to buy your building on Center Street."

"Which one? I have three."

"The old book store."

"What for?"

"I'm moving back to Palmerton. I need a place to live and room for a studio. I'll have both in the bookstore."

The silence stretched out while Maive pinned her with a narrowed gaze.

"You're not going to turn it into some fancy gallery and have all kinds of snotty, artsy folk swarming the center of town, are you?"

An image of Evan's exclusive Park Ave gallery filled her mind. What fun Charles would have with Maive's description of his world. Biting back a laugh, she shook her head. "No. I have no interest in opening my own gallery. I'm committed to one in Manhattan already. I just need a place to live and work."

"Okay."

Cara blinked at the curt agreement. "Okay?"

"That's what I said, isn't it? You have a hearing problem?"

Her gaze swung to a stunned Jill before resettling on Maive. "Just like that?"

"You want the property or don't you? It won't be cheap."

"I want it!" Cara leaned forward in her chair, repeating for good measure. "I definitely want it."

A door slammed at the back of the house and Maive turned toward the hallway. "Is that you, boy?"

Heavy footsteps moved in their direction. Both

Cara and Jill followed Maive's gaze.

"All done, old lady," a deep, male voice answered a moment before a set of broad shoulders leaned around the doorjamb. Above a taunting white smile, piercing blue eyes swept the room and Cara jerked upright in her chair. All disturbingly muscled male perfection and smiling charm, Michael Finnegan immediately straightened to fill the doorway.

She swallowed painfully, dismayed at the chaos erupting in her belly as his intent gaze tangled with hers.

"Ladies." He nodded and thankfully looked away.

The low timbre of his voice brushed across her already stretched nerve endings and left goose bumps behind. Her eyes followed helplessly as he crossed the room, stopping beside the settee. He bent at the waist, dropping a kiss on Maive's forehead.

Cara stared incredulously at the tool belt slung low on his lean hips.

"You can do back flips off that step now, Maive."

Maive sniffed. "I may just try that tomorrow. You see if I don't."

He chuckled and straightened to his full six-five height. When he turned, the dimpled grin, captured on the covers of all those magazines, curved his lips. He lowered a hip to the arm of the settee, propping an elbow on one thigh, and turned to Jill.

"Hi, Jill. I saw that boy of yours pitch last week. He's got a mean fast ball."

Cara watched, disgusted, as Jill reacted to the mega-wattage of his bigger-than-life personality. Her fingers fluttered over her perfect hairdo. Eyes twinkling, she returned Finn's smile.

"He loves the game and Doug is beside himself with pride," she said of her husband. "He has dreams of watching him play in the big leagues."

"Finn." Maive bumped his thigh with an elbow. "Have you met Mary O'Shea's middle daughter, Cara?"

Cobalt blue beams shifted to Cara, and she nearly cringed at the palpable memory shining in them. His smile easy, he spoke in a subtle rumble.

"We've had the pleasure. Hello, Cara."

"Hello." Fighting the flush of remembered humiliation heating her cheeks, she returned the greeting stiffly. She slid her gaze back to Maive, and relative safety. The old lady came to her rescue, craning her neck to aim a sly smile up at Finn.

"I just sold her the old book store."

Finn's head whipped around.

"You sold it?" He popped up from his slouched position, his back going poker straight. "I tried to buy it from you not two months ago. You said it wasn't for sale."

"It wasn't, then."

"But it is now?" Icy intenseness replaced his charming smile. "How much do you want for it?"

Maive cackled a laugh. "You'll have to ask the O'Shea girl. She owns it now."

Calculation hardened his features when he turned to study Cara.

She was at a complete loss. Technically, she hadn't bought the place. She didn't even know what she'd have to pay for it. Yet for some reason, known only to Maive Cataldo, the old lady was having the time of her life, denying Finn the property.

Far be it from her to contradict the dragon lady. A

burst of satisfied excitement cooled the heated flush on Cara's cheeks. The bookstore was hers and she'd be keeping it. She informed him of that fact before he could open his mouth. "It's not for sale."

Maive's wrinkled face twisted into a satisfied smirk, and she nodded her approval.

"That's just wrong, Maive."

Maive dismissed his grumbled complaint with the wave of a gnarled hand. "You'd have it for a simple investment property. You have plenty of those. The girl needs a place to work and to lay her head. She's a famous artist now, you know. She needs a good working space."

Cara met his frown with a lift of her chin and a satisfied smile that said *that's right, pal*.

Rising from the arm of the settee, he crossed tanned, well-muscled arms over his equally impressive chest. He settled into a cocky stance with his weight resting on one hip.

"Ryan said you were in town for his and Erin's wedding. I'm his best man. We'll be walking together." The smile died on her lips. "He didn't mention you've come back for good." Trepidation tickled her spine when his smile widened and his blue laser eyes ran over her contemplatively. "Welcome back to Palmerton, neighbor."

Chapter Three

Damn, she was beautiful.

Seeing her again verified what he'd noted at their chance meeting in Manhattan, several years earlier. Cara O'Shea had grown up, and maturity only increased the beauty with which she'd been blessed.

Even as a teenager, she had a certain something. A powerful, invisible force, like irresistible pheromones reaching out to grab a man by the libido. And it wasn't just her looks, though damn...her height alone would draw attention. Six-foot beauties were hard to ignore, but beyond her height and sultry allure, she emitted a shy innocence that tugged at a man's protective instincts, urging him to wrap her in his arms and keep her safe.

Her dark auburn hair, piled atop her head in a messy knot, made his fingers itch to plunge into the fiery curls. Her large eyes, as green as an antique pop bottle, could cause a man to forget what he was saying. They dominated her stunning face and the flash of dismay in them, when he told Maive they'd met, tugged at the memory of their first meeting, nearly a decade earlier.

Her eyes flashed with a similar panic that day as rivulets of pool water splashed to the deck from her nearly transparent dress. She'd been beautiful then, too.

Beautiful and scared.

The idiot high school boys surrounding him hadn't noticed the fear. Not that he could blame them. There wasn't a man alive, young or old, who wouldn't have been blinded by the magnificence of her tender young body, shivering in the late spring air.

Hell, he'd already been a man full grown, and she just a girl, and yet he hadn't been able to look away from her bring-a-man-to-his-knees body. When his bewitched mind finally cleared enough to note the cruel taunts of the young men, he was disgusted, with them and himself. And when she met his gaze across the distance of the pool, the terror and humiliation in her eyes made him want to strangle someone.

Little more than a child, she faced an unbearable embarrassment with a quiet dignity he'd never forgotten. Married at the time, he wouldn't have done anything about the instant attraction churning in his gut, even if he had been single. She was just a kid, after all. But, she wasn't a kid now.

Though she'd all but stolen the bookstore right out from under his nose, he knew where to lay the blame. The building's Central Street location made it ideal for a youth community center. If he had told Maive what he had in mind, she would have sold to him no questions asked. But, as usual, he'd been enjoying the cat and mouse maneuvering with his strong willed great-aunt. Selling to someone else was a move he never anticipated.

The girl who stared down a mob of idiotic teenage boys wouldn't be an easy nut to crack, and from the satisfied gleam in her eyes, convincing the woman she'd become to give up the bookstore was a long shot.

Still, he welcomed the quickening of his pulse. Romancing the beautiful artist, with an eye toward winning back his building was a challenge he couldn't resist.

****

"Did you know Michael Finnegan was Ryan Espizitto's cousin *and* his best man?"

Across the booth, Meggy Calhoun paused with her slice of pizza midair. "Actually, I did."

"Were you going to tell me, or were you just going to let me walk in blind to the fact that I am going to have to put up with him for several hours on Saturday?"

Her friend's pixie like face contorted in a grimace. "Not to mention Friday night at the rehearsal dinner."

Cara dropped her head into her hands.

Meggy leaned on her elbows. "By the way, I won't be there Friday night. We're short staffed. I have to work."

Cara groaned.

"It won't be that bad, Cara."

"He was there that night, Meggy." Cara glanced up, hoping the familiar haunting the memory delivered didn't show in her eyes.

"There were a lot of people there. Besides, it was a long time ago. He probably doesn't remember."

She would like to believe that, but couldn't. She never told Meggy about bumping into Finn shortly before his divorce, but like every other encounter she had with Palmerton's football hero, the meeting left a lasting impression. She'd been too flustered to notice at the time, but he had greeted her by name that night.

And she knew exactly *when* he'd learned her name.

Without ever having met, never having spoken a

word, she and Finn shared the second worst moment of her life. The worst moment happened only hours earlier, on the afternoon of her high school graduation, when she spotted her father slipping into the motel on the edge of town with his secretary, Hannah Dunn.

Heartsick, and wanting nothing more than to find a quiet place to cry out her broken heart, she let Meggy convince her to go ahead with their plans to visit several graduation parties that evening. Though she'd always avoided the drunken gatherings the other kids claimed were so much fun, she gulped down the first beer someone handed her and by the time they arrived at Brad Murphy's back yard, she was more than a little tipsy.

At Meggy's heels, she passed through the open gate, following her friend to one of the tables by the edge of the pool where several friends were seated. Meggy sat, immediately drawn into conversation. Swaying a bit, Cara stood to the side, her gaze roaming the raucous crowd. Her eyes immediately caught on a dark head of blue-black hair beyond the pool, rising above the surrounding group of teenage boys.

Her heart fluttered wildly in her chest, and a familiar flock of butterflies took flight in her belly. From the age of eleven, she'd lived for glimpses of Palmerton's famous football hero. When he'd left town after graduation, she followed his college career and hadn't missed a game or interview once he'd been drafted by Tampa and had gone pro, but three years had passed since she'd seen him in person.

The gray Boston College T-shirt stretched across his powerful chest and showcased the mouthwatering musculature of his tanned biceps. His long legs were encased in a pair of time-faded jeans and his face, when he turned her way, was still the most beautiful she'd ever seen.

Caught up in the sheer joy of soaking up the sight of a live and in person Finn, she jolted when a hand landed on her arm. Her balance impaired, she staggered. Big hands caught her, holding her steady. She blinked up into the eyes of Timmy Faulkner, the bane of her high school existence.

"Whoa there. Living up to your name tonight, Cara Cups?"

His sneering smile made her stomach churn, and her voice came out a husky whisper. "Leave me alone."

His rough fingers, wrapped around her arms, made her skin crawl. She twisted in an effort to free herself. He let her struggle for a moment, leaning closer. Shuddering at the thought of bodily contact, she stumbled back a step. His eyes flashed with cruel intent as he released her with a quick shove.

Her arms cart-wheeled and the ground beneath her feet suddenly vanished. She landed with a cold splash. Moments later, she surfaced in the pool to find Timmy standing on the deck, bent at the waist, beside himself with laughter.

"Help her out!"

Meggy's furious demand echoed through the now silent party. Two sets of male hands grasped Cara beneath the arms and wrenched her out of the water. Her rescuers set her on her feet, where she stood dripping and shivering.

"Are you okay, Cara?"

She couldn't answer, despite the concern in Meggy's voice. All around Brad Murphy's back yard, avid faces stared at Cara. The party had come to a complete standstill. Even the music seemed to have quieted.

Horrified, her gaze flew to the corner of the patio where Finn stood. Sure enough, his blue laser eyes met hers as if he'd been waiting for her to turn his way.

She couldn't breathe, couldn't escape his steady stare until, through the buzz in her ears, the first snickering exclamation rocked her back on her heels.

"Now, those are tits!"

She tore her gaze from Finn's to glance down, then wanted to vanish into the brick deck at her feet. The thin material of her pretty, yellow sundress stuck to her body like filmy, transparent skin. Her lacy silk bra and panties may as well have been invisible for all the modesty they provided.

A strangled cry escaped, despite her clenched teeth, and she plucked at the clinging material. Seconds later, she gave up the useless effort. Desperate, she attempted to cover strategic spots with her hands, even as her mind registered the mocking comments of *Cara Cups* and *porn star*.

Meggy snapped into action. Shoving passed the still laughing Timmy, she knocked him into the pool on her way to the closest football player to demand his player's jacket. When Cara's furious friend returned to bundle her into the coat, Cara couldn't stop herself from looking back at Finn.

No expression showed on his face, but his blue eyes blazed with the same undisguised lust as the boys surrounding him. Still and unblinking, his eyes burned in the midst of laughter, the jabbing of elbows, and crude observations.

While Meggy zipped Cara into the warm jacket like a hovering mother, a chill washed over her, having nothing to do with temperature and everything to do with the layer of ice forming around her battered dignity. No stranger to taunting insults from the boys at school, she steeled her heart against the humiliating remarks buzzing around her like angry bees. Chin held high, she refused to let any of them, including Finn, see her cringe with embarrassment.

Instead, she let her eyes go frigid, and welcomed the death of each and every one of those butterflies she'd carried within her for years. Dragging her gaze from Finn's, she swept the rest of the crowd with a disdainful glance, before turning and walking away. She'd left town two days later, and with the exception of the occasional, quick, turnaround visit, she hadn't looked back.

The events of that day destroyed her childhood self. She'd done her best to put the memories behind her, but she couldn't ever forget, neither her father's betrayal, *nor* her humiliation beside that pool. And from the shadows in Finn's eyes in Maive's parlor, he hadn't forgotten either.

Not that it mattered. *Some* good came of the events of that long ago day and night. She emerged from the experience with a new to-hell-with-them-all attitude and while she occasionally mourned the trusting girl she left behind, she no longer tolerated anyone's crap.

In the past eight years, she'd faced down bigger obstacles than Finn the Fine, and triumphed. No longer a shy seventeen-year-old in a transparent dress, she would survive sharing rubber chicken and toasts with the town stud, even if it killed her.

Chapter Four

"There'll be swimming after the rehearsal. Don't forget your suit." Erin's voice carried up the stairwell to Cara's childhood bedroom in her mother's house.

In a singsong voice, Cara called back. "I don't think so."

"But everyone will be swimming. You *have* to bring your suit."

She leaned close to the mirror to attach a dangling earring, mumbling, "Not in this lifetime." Makeup applied lightly, she wore her dark auburn hair down. It fell in riotous curls down her back. The long, floral, sheath dress was one of her favorites. She loved the dark green color, and the way the loose material muted the impact of her curves.

Grabbing her purse, she hurried downstairs.

Frustrated, yet gorgeous, Erin paced the hallway with her hands on her hips, her petite frame displayed to perfection in white linen drawstring pants and a fuchsia tank. A large tote hung from one shoulder. Her strawberry blonde hair was slicked back in a sophisticated knot, and her lips were pulled tight in a mulish frown.

"Don't start." Cara brushed by her.

Erin followed her outside, the heels of her sandals clicking on the walkway. "You always say that."

"And you never listen. We'll take my new car." Cara stopped beside the dark Jeep Cherokee she'd purchased immediately upon landing back in Boston. She grinned across the hood and opened the door. "In case I need to escape."

Erin slipped into the passenger seat with a huff. "I want you to have a good time tonight, Cara."

With Daddy and *Michael Finnegan in attendance? Fat chance!* But she wasn't about to ruin her sister's night, so she tried to reassure her.

"I will. I promise. I just don't have any interest in frolicking around in a pool with a bunch of strangers."

"They're not strangers." Erin turned in her seat, her eyes pleading. "The town's not that big. You'll know most of them."

"*You'll* know most of them. I know many of the people in town by sight, not because we were friendly. I spent the majority of my childhood buried in the art department or with my nose in a book. Besides, I've been gone a long time."

"Exactly," Erin persisted. "But you're back now and I want you to be happy so you'll stay. You could make a few new friends tonight, if you let yourself."

Cara laughed at Erin's earnest expression. Her outgoing sister barreled through life, collecting people the way other women collected shoes, and whenever possible, took steps to see everyone else did the same. However, her tactics never worked with Cara.

"Relax, mommy. I have plenty of friends and I'm home to stay."

Erin's forehead wrinkled with a sheepish smile. "I'm hovering again, aren't I?"

Cara patted her hand where it rested on top of her

tote. "Yes, you are, but I love you anyway."

Her sister chattered her excitement while Cara inhaled a deep breath to relax. Though wired from this morning's meeting with Maive, she was also tired, and the idea of seeing Daddy tonight had her more anxious than she wanted to admit. And running into Finn in Maive's parlor hadn't helped.

What the hell was an ex-pro quarterback with a Super Bowl ring, a recurring spot on the Sunday morning sports shows, and a half dozen lucrative marketing contracts doing fixing an old lady's steps? A tool belt, for crying out loud! The man looked like a six-foot five Mr. June in a hunk-of-the-month calendar.

His thick, black hair was longer than she ever remembered it being, finger-combed back from his broad forehead. The rough shadow of his chiseled jaw, darkened with a day's growth of stubble, only increased the piercing blue of his eyes. Much to her chagrin, his body hadn't gone to pot since he retired from professional sports. He still sported the superbly muscled form that had always made her heart flutter and throb.

And what was she doing, noticing how well his jeans fit his tight butt when he leaned to brush a kiss on Maive's forehead? God, she must have some kind of hormonal imbalance when it came to Michael Finnegan. She was as bad as the countless women, hanging all over him on the covers of those rag magazines.

And damn it, she knew better. She hadn't talked to Daddy in years for precisely the same reason she shouldn't be noticing the breadth of Finn's shoulders, straining the material of his T-shirt. She'd witnessed firsthand the kind of man he was *and* what he thought of his wedding vows that night she bumped into him in Manhattan.

Well, she had become a master at ignoring big, hunky men. Hadn't Charles told her so on more than one occasion? All she had to do was make it through the rehearsal dinner tonight, and the wedding tomorrow, and then she'd be home free.

A group of men were tossing a football on the lawn of Ryan's parent's sprawling ranch house when they arrived. She heaved a relieved sigh that Finn wasn't among them. Ryan broke away from the impromptu game to jog over and pull his fiancée from the passenger side.

His light blond hair glinted in the afternoon sunlight and his hazel eyes gleamed with love as he smiled down into Erin's beaming face. Sweeping her into his arms, he kissed her hungrily to the hoots and whistles of the other men.

Cara grabbed Erin's bag and climbed from the vehicle as the men wandered over. Ducking her head, she busied herself by tucking her keys inside her purse. God, she hated this kind of thing, but remaining invisible in the face of strange men had never been possible and the need to do so was a behavior she'd fought long and hard to overcome. A few days back in Palmerton and she was reverting to form. That wouldn't do. With a deep breath, she lifted her chin and rounded the hood of the Jeep.

Ryan dropped his arm from Erin's shoulders to hug Cara in greeting. She'd worn her flats tonight and looked her sister's six-foot fiancé in the eye. A wide grin spread across his handsome face.

"Welcome to the family."

"Isn't that my line?" Cara teased with a small smile.

A towering wall of males suddenly surrounded Erin, passing her from one to the next for sloppy kisses. When they began to pass her around for seconds, Ryan snatched her to his side.

"Get your own," he growled in false affront.

Cara couldn't help but smile, even as four sets of laughing male eyes turned to her. There a time when, faced with looming males, she would have frozen in awkward fear. Instead, the smile remained on her face as Ryan made the introductions.

"This is Erin's sister, Cara. Cara, my cousins. Mathew, Austin, Tony." He jerked his thumb toward the youngest of the men. "And the shrimp there is Paul."

"Hello." Cara's eyes moved over the group without pausing on anyone in particular. She'd been right. She knew all but the youngest by sight.

"I think I may *have* just found my own." The tallest of the group captured her hand. Sandy blond hair capped a handsome face with faded blue eyes. The family resemblance was evident in his crooked smile.

"Get in line, Matt."

Cara jumped and didn't need to spin around to know who had spoken. Finn's deep voice set off a ripple of goose flesh that caused the fine hair on her arms to stand on end, and several sensitive body parts to pucker.

Forget hormonal imbalance. Michael Finnegan was more like a virus. She tugged her hand, but Matt held her fingers firm.

"I saw her first." Matt frowned.

"No, you didn't." Humor permeated Finn's easy response.

Matt's frown flattened into a scowl, and she took advantage of his loosening fingers to free her hand. She shot an annoyed frown at Erin.

"Quit it, you two. You're embarrassing my sister." Erin tucked her arm through Cara's, tugging her toward the front door. "Sorry." She rolled her eyes at Cara then glanced back at the group of men following them up the front lawn. "I'd forgotten the effect you have on the weaker sex."

Cara laughed. "Lighten up, little sister. I've learned a thing or two over the years. They don't bother me." And they didn't. Well, except for the viral Finn. Her laughter died.

Maybe she should begin taking antibiotics.

The mouthwatering smell of roasting beef scented the air of the back yard. Cries of greeting rose for the arriving bride. Erin introduced Cara to Ryan's parents. A handsome couple, the Espizittos' affection for her baby sister gained them Cara's undying appreciation.

Erin then pointed out various Espizitto family members. Cara was surprised to find Maive holding court at one of the linen covered tables scattered about the expanse of lawn. Great Aunt Maive nodded in greeting.

Cara shook her head. Small towns. Nearly everyone was related somehow. And that explained why Finn was fixing Maive's back step.

Mary O'Shea and Shan, Cara and Erin's older sister, sat at a table beyond the patio with Shan's two young boys. Cara wiggled her fingers at her nephews, taking the glass of wine someone handed her while Erin jabbered on about wedding details to one of the female guests.

As though sensing his presence, Cara turned to find Finn several feet away. He ambled by with a football tucked under one arm and a group of teen boys at his heels. His deep blue gaze swept from the top of her head to her painted toenails.

"Nice." His quiet murmur made her bristle.

She gave him a tight smile and turned away, pretending interest in Erin's ongoing discussion of her wedding centerpieces.

When Cara eventually joined Mary and Shan at the table, her father still hadn't appeared. She began to relax as the meal was served, laughing along with everyone else at the barbed jibes and teasing toasts for the engaged couple, until a flash of tension dimmed her mother's eyes. Knowing what she would find, she followed Mary's gaze.

Tom O'Shea spoke quietly to Ryan's father at the far edge of the patio. Erin joined them, greeting Tom with a tight hug. Cara laid her hand over Mary's. Across the table, Shan smiled tightly and shrugged her shoulders. She followed her boys as they raced off to greet grandpa.

Cara remained where she was.

Unfortunately, all too soon, Ryan's mother called for the members of the wedding party to line up for a quick rehearsal. Cara stood and sent Mary a forced smile. Shan stepped to Cara's side and linked their arms, crossing the lawn to where the others gathered.

"She's okay."

Cara tossed a glance over her shoulder at Mary.

"She doesn't look okay."

Shan sighed. "It's just the wedding atmosphere stirring up memories. She and Daddy worked things out a long time ago."

In her head, Cara knew what Shan said was true, but her heart didn't understand. Mary, Erin, and Shan had all forgiven Tom for what he'd done and had pressed her to do the same over the years. It was an old argument, one bound to come up with increased frequency now that she was back in town. She knew they all considered today a first step toward healing the rift between her and her father, but she just wanted to get the uncomfortable meeting over with.

Shan squeezed her arm as they approached the gathered members of the wedding party. Erin waited with Tom at her side. While her sister's smile was pleading, Tom's was hopeful.

"Hello, Daddy." Cara's reluctant greeting came out stilted.

"Cara mine."

Seemingly unfazed by the coolness of her greeting, he gathered her to his broad chest, holding her tight even when she didn't return his embrace. She turned her head, her arms hanging limply at her sides, and met the intense gaze of Finn several feet away. She flushed with embarrassment and dropped her gaze. Tom pressed a kiss to the top of her head, releasing her only when she forced the issue by stepping back.

She could have kissed the Espizitto's pastor when he cleared his throat and began instructing everyone on their responsibilities in the proceedings, beginning with Tom. She heaved a cleansing breath when he reluctantly turned away.

Unfortunately, her relief was short lived. The members of the party began to pair up according to their place in the procession. Finn appeared at her side. He offered her his arm and with her nerves stretched to the breaking point, she accepted, linking hers through his.

They spent the next twenty minutes running through the process twice. A round of applause and laughter went up when Ryan kissed his future bride. Cara waited until the party members began wandering off toward their tables to make her excuses to leave to a disappointed Erin and Ryan, then slipped back to her table to hug Mary, Shan and the boys. Avoiding Tom where he stood with several men under a towering oak, she made her way through the tables toward the side gate.

"Running away?" Finn's deep, softly challenging voice brought her feet to a hesitant stop. She turned chilled eyes on him where he sat with a quiet, watchful Maive.

"Simply calling it a night."

A single black brow arched in response. She lifted her chin, daring him to call her a liar.

"Leave the girl be, boy. She's no coward. She's just confused."

Maive's wise blue eyes held compassionate understanding. Cara longed to say something easy and carefree, and put a lie to Maive's truth, but she couldn't seem to make her mouth work. Instead, she swallowed convulsively on the sudden desire to weep.

Finn frowned and pushed back his chair as if to rise. Maive forestalled him with a gnarled hand on his forearm.

"Come by Monday morning, Cara O'Shea. We'll sign those papers."

Cara nodded, and did exactly what Michael Finnegan accused her of doing. She ran.

Chapter Five

A ferocious thunderstorm blew through town an hour before the wedding service, leaving the day sweltering hot and steamy. The fan cooling system in the church was no match for the oppressive heat, and by the time the newlyweds signed the marriage certificate and the last pictures were taken, the men had removed their jackets and the woman were fanning themselves with whatever they could find. The coolness of the air conditioning was a welcome relief when the wedding party arrived at the reception hall.

Finn noticed Cara's pallor the moment she exited the ladies' room, and when Tom O'Shea's new wife, Hannah, emerged a moment later, he knew the reason. His gaze followed as Cara made her way across the dance floor to find a seat at Mary O'Shea's side. Though her tension was evident, he enjoyed the unconsciously sensual movement of Cara's curvy body in the incredible, pale yellow bridesmaid's dress she wore.

Even from a distance, the smile she gave her mother appeared strained. She tucked the youngest of Shan's boys to her side, nuzzling his flushed cheeks. Brian laughed and tried to squirm from her hold, but the affection between aunt and nephew was evident.

Finn's gaze swung to Tom, standing at the bar. The

older man watched Cara as well. Focused on his middle daughter, a wistful sadness clouded his eyes.

While Finn wasn't privy to the details surrounding the rift between Cara and Tom O'Shea, the reason for their estrangement was common knowledge around Palmerton. Erin and Shan seemed to have moved beyond Tom's infidelity, coming to terms with their parents' four-year-old divorce, and Tom's second marriage. Obviously, Cara hadn't.

The memory of the tears shimmering in her beautiful eyes before she'd fled the rehearsal dinner bothered him. He hardly knew the woman, but her distress stayed with him, long after the party wound down.

Of their own accord, his eyes sought her out once again. She was a puzzle he wanted to get his hands on, but since his own divorce, he had a self-imposed policy against becoming involved with anyone or anything even resembling long term. And despite her party girl looks and bunny-of-the-month body, Tom O'Shea's daughter reeked of permanence.

Joining Cara when the band called for the wedding party's first dance, he found himself searching for a temporary loophole in his policy.

****

Cara slid into Finn's embrace, and he guided her about the dance floor with flawless ease. She should have known he'd be a graceful dancer. His fluid moves on the gridiron were legendary. She had watched them most of her life.

Eventually, the gentle sway of the music relaxed her, and she began to enjoy the dance, until he drew her closer to avoid bumping into the newlyweds. She immediately stiffened her shoulders, but if he noticed her reaction when her body brushed against his from breasts to thighs, he ignored it. He held her close and spun them away.

When he ducked his head to nuzzle her hairline, she decided he *had* noticed. He took full advantage by murmuring in her ear. "You smell great."

She gritted her teeth. "Back off, Finnegan."

Her attempt to put some distance between them, by pushing at his shoulder, gained no results. He held her tight.

"Lighten up, O'Shea. It was a compliment. I like your hair down." He tilted his head to peer into her eyes as he rumbled his absurd comment. "The way you wore it last night."

Mere inches separated her face from his and her lips tightened in annoyance. Did he actually expect her to respond to that? Stick to the plan, Cara. Ignore him. She stared blankly over his shoulder.

"All those wild curls beg a man to sink his fingers in to see if they're as soft as they appear."

Her mouth twitched with the need to respond. Okay, maybe someone who'd spent his life being slammed to the ground by three-hundred pound behemoths wasn't capable of reading the subtleties of body language. He probably had his brain scrambled so often he needed verbal cues to understand not all women appreciated his brand of juvenile machismo.

"You know, Finnegan," she spoke nonchalantly, staring straight ahead as though he didn't bother her at all. "There are medications that can help lessen the mental complications of brain damage from repeated concussions. Someone in the front office of the NFL should be able to give you the name of a doctor who can prescribe them."

He chuckled, and she made the mistake of shifting her eyes back to his. They twinkled with mirth above a bright, white smile. The riotous fluttering in her belly brought a slight rush of nausea. Dismayed to discover those damn butterflies weren't dead after all, she looked away. *Was brain damage contagious?*

"How much do you want for the bookstore?"

She blinked, jerking her gaze back to his at the sudden change in subject. "It's not for sale."

"Everything is for sale, if the price is right."

"Not everything."

"How did you convince Maive to sell to you?"

"I didn't have to convince her. I told her I wanted it and she agreed."

"I've been after her to sell me the bookstore for two years, but she wasn't interested."

Her smile brittle, she suggested, "Maybe she just doesn't like you."

He threw back his head and laughed. She stared at the strong cords of his throat, annoyed at the shimmer of heat coursing through her.

"She loves me." His boast was thick with utter confidence.

"Obviously not enough to sell you the bookstore."

He dipped his head to meet her eyes. "I would have charmed her into it eventually. You beat me to the punch."

She rolled her eyes at his arrogance, and he grinned, his crooked smile producing killer dimples. No doubt, he would have gotten his way with Maive in time.

"It always amazes me how men like you can walk upright, carrying around such a big head."

The grin remained on his face. "Men like me?"

She smirked. "Good looking jocks with more brawn than brain."

He ignored the insult to his intelligence, his grin widening. "You think I'm good looking, huh? Why don't we slip out of here and go somewhere private where you can tell me more?"

Well, she walked right into that one, hadn't she? She lowered her eyes, turning her head to stare blindly at the other dancers. "You've just made my point."

He released her hand to grasp her chin between his index finger and thumb, turning her until she was facing him again.

"I was kidding, Cara." She didn't return his smile. "Okay, maybe not completely," he admitted in a teasing tone.

She made her stare blank.

"Jesus, you're skittish." The song ended and she scowled at him when he didn't immediately let her go. "I'm attracted to you, O'Shea."

If it wouldn't have drawn attention to the heat flushing up her chest and into her face, she would have slapped her hands over her cheeks. She miscalculated, believing ignoring him would dissuade him from pursuing the interest she read in his eyes. But how could she dissuade him if he refused to be ignored and swallowed her insults with a smile?

The uninterested bitch tactic always worked for her in the past. Well, mostly. But no cutesy insults would do the trick this time. Bold truth was called for.

"I'm not interested."

His gaze on hers remained steady. His big hand on the small of her back and his grasp on her chin kept her from making a cutting exit. Her eyes darted about the room searching for an escape route. When she didn't find one, she finally glanced back at him. His eyes held a touch of wry humor.

"We'll see about that."

She attempted to jerk back from the mouth descending toward hers, but he held her chin firm. His lips barely brushed hers in a chaste kiss, before he straightened.

"Thanks for the dance, O'Shea." He dropped his hand from her chin and walked away, leaving her staring after him from the middle of the dance floor.

With Meggy's assistance, she managed to avoid him the rest of the evening, until he stopped to say goodbye to the newlyweds. Standing at the bar with her sisters and Meggy, Cara remained silent as he explained he needed to catch the last shuttle out of Logan Airport, to tape a guest interview in the morning on the Sport's Network. She refused to blush when he shot her a grinning wink before leaving, and then did her best to ignore Meggy's raised brows.

Without his disturbing presence, she was able to relax and enjoy the rest of the reception, with the exception of the few minutes guided around the dance floor in her father's arms. Erin proved her skills at manipulating a situation to achieve her goals, by asking Cara to dance with Ryan, while she moved about the floor with Tom.

After working her way close, Erin spun out of Tom's arms, and without a word, was swept into Ryan's. The newlyweds abandoned Cara and her father standing in the middle of the crowd of dancers. Cara glared at Erin over Tom's shoulder, to no avail. Her sneaky sister shrugged her shoulders, smiled pleadingly, and danced away in the arms of her new husband.

Uncomfortably aware of the curious eyes watching them, Cara had no choice but to take the hand Tom held out to her.

"I hear you bought the old bookstore." He spoke quietly as they moved about the wooden floor. "Congratulations. You were always too much like me to be happy for long in the big city. Palmerton is more your style."

"I don't consider being like you a ringing endorsement."

Under her hand, the telltale stiffening of his shoulder muscles made her belly clench in self-reproach. She flushed, cursing the temper fueling her nasty tongue. Erin's wedding was neither the time, nor the place, for a skirmish in their decade old, cold war. She sucked in a bracing breath.

"Thanks to Evan Malone's invaluable guidance, my work is selling well. I no longer have reason to stay in Manhattan when I can work right here." She couldn't help adding a dig. "Besides, Ma needs me."

He didn't react to her barb the way she expected. He only nodded.

"She loves you. Your being home again means more to her than you know."

How would you know, she wanted to demand. She clenched her teeth to keep her mouth shut. How dare he act as though he cared what Ma thought or felt? He'd thrown away that right to be with his precious Hannah.

Cara would have moved away when the song came to an end, but he held her hand.

"I'm glad you're home, too, Cara mine."

She tugged her hand free. His arms fell to his sides. "I...I was hoping we could talk sometime. Maybe have lunch?"

She didn't know how to respond. The man she'd idolized her entire childhood stood in front of her, his eyes pleading for understanding, yet all she could see was the memory of his hand, reaching out to his mistress in front of Harper's Motel.

But despite the bitter resentment the memory stirred, she couldn't stand to see the near desperation in his eyes. Her gaze skittered away and landed on Maive Cataldo at a nearby table. Her blue eyes sparkled with unspoken challenge. Cara could practically hear the dragon lady demanding, "Well, are you going to answer the man, Cara O'Shea?"

"I'll let you know" was the best she could offer him. She stalked off, ignoring Maive's satisfied smile.

Chapter Six

It would be several days before the property was officially hers, but the bookstore already provided a sense of home. Cara could hardly contain her excitement when the moving truck pulled down the back alley, and two burly, young men unloaded her things. Several days of hard work had the tiny upstairs apartment organized and livable. Downstairs was another story.

Determined, she stood at the edge of what would eventually hold her studio and glared at the stacked crates containing her art supplies. Pulling a crowbar from the toolbox she had dragged downstairs, she went to work. Two hours later, cleaning solutions and thinners filled the shelving along one wall beside boxes of pigment and sorted brushes. She stored canvases of various sizes behind the counter where the book store's register used to sit.

With an easel tucked under one arm, she swiped her brow with a bare forearm. The glare of the late afternoon sunlight pouring through the wall of windows along the front of the building was so bright it hurt the eyes, and heated the room while the air-conditioner battled valiantly to retain a bearable temperature. Despite the sleeveless tank top and shorts she wore, she was sweating like a pig.

No wonder the bookstore failed. The electric bill alone would have put even the most thriving business into financial trouble.

But, she'd already addressed that particular problem. At Mary's suggestion, she ordered custom shutters for the ceiling high panes. The salesman who came to measure the order promised they would be installed by the end of the week. Studying the high ceiling, she mentally added a couple of ceiling fans to her ever-growing list.

She was still deciding just how many it would take to keep her from drowning in her own sweat, when the front door opened. Spinning around, the easel under her arm swept a box of pigment from the top of an open crate, sending it crashing to the floor.

Silhouetted by the late afternoon light as he stood in the doorway, his face in shadow, she recognized Finn's muscular frame. Her already unpleasant mood soured to aggravation.

"Ever heard of knocking?" She opened the easel, setting it to its feet, and bent to lift the box of pigment, shoving it onto one of the shelves.

He closed the door behind him. "When was the last time you knocked on the door of a business before going inside?"

"This isn't a business. It's my studio *and* home."

"I stand corrected."

She gritted her teeth at his reasonable tone and the damned crooked smile spreading over his face. Typically gorgeous in a pair of faded jeans and a crisp white T-shirt, he appeared cool and completely at ease. In comparison, she resembled a wet rag, and she certainly wasn't cool. The temperature in the room shot up ten degrees with his arrival. She would remember to lock the door from now on.

When he didn't say anything else, she blew out an impatient sigh. "Was there something you needed?"

He shook his head. "Nope." He crossed his arms. The patient smile remained on his face. "Maive said you wanted to talk to me."

"Maive? Why would Maive...?" Cara spied the tape measure clipped to his low slung waist band, and her stomach performed a crazy roll. Oh, no. No, no, no! He couldn't be the carpenter Maive promised to send her way. The fickle fates couldn't be that vicious.

He chuckled as though sensing her dawning horror. "Carpentry is a hobby of mine."

Her gaze flew to the built-in shelving before snapping back to him. "*You* did the original renovation?"

"Some of my finest work, if I do say so myself."

Well, damn. With her stomach plummeting, her gaze ran lovingly over the exquisite woodwork throughout the room. He had reason to brag, and she would just have to find some other handyman with a tool belt to complete the changes she had planned. No way did she want Michael Finnegan under foot for however long the renovations took. She'd hire someone from Manhattan first.

"I don't think..."

He brushed passed her to make his way further into the room, leaving her talking to his back.

Running a big hand over the wood of one of the freestanding shelves lining the center of the room, he glanced over his shoulder. "You'll want to open up the place, and you won't need these. I know someone who'll be happy to take them off your hands."

"Now, wait a minute." She scrambled after him when he continued toward the back of the building.

"There's a summer camp north of here," he continued as though she hadn't spoken. "They take in troubled kids. I know the administrator would jump at the chance to expand the small library they have on site."

"I...of course they can have them."

"You'll want to do something with the flooring. There's hardwood beneath the carpeting. The bookstore owner put in carpeting to keep down the noise, but the floor was in good shape. It shouldn't take much to revert the wood to its original form." He continued through the aisles toward the rear of the building.

Realizing she was following him like a lost puppy, she stopped short. "Hey!"

He stopped and turned, raising one dark brow.

"I'm not hiring you." With a bland stare, she crossed her arms.

"Why not?"

Why not? She wasn't going to get into why not with him. And what kind of question was that anyway? She didn't want to hire him and that was all he needed to know.

"Because, I don't want to."

"Well, that's a stupid reason." Humor danced in his blue eyes.

She sputtered incoherently.

"Look." He spoke before she could find some actual words with which to blast him. "You've bought the building, so I have to believe you'll want any changes done properly. It's a great old place and a piece of history in this town. I did the original renovation. You're going to want continuity with the work already completed. That means hiring me."

Her disbelieving snort was loud in the quiet building. "Any contractor worthy of the name can give me continuity. You just don't want anyone else getting their hands on what you've already built here."

Twin dimples popped with his grin. "There is that."

"I don't think so."

"I'll tell you what," he proposed, as though she hadn't already made her decision. "Tell me what you want done, and I'll write up a bid. If you still don't want me doing the work…" Irritation seeped into his tone. "I'll give you the name of someone who won't screw up what's already done."

That he was studying the woodwork like a proud parent worried over their only child, was the only reason she didn't refuse his suggestion outright.

Frustration made her voice sharp. "Don't you have some sneaker or athletic wear to peddle? I don't just want cosmetic work done here, Finnegan. It's going to take some time to get this place looking the way I want it."

"My schedule is flexible."

The humor in his eyes grated on her already stretched nerves. "I want walls taken out, windows put in. Aren't you afraid you'll be too tired to devote time to finding the next bimbo to share the limelight with you on the cover of one of those magazines?"

God, she sounded like a bitch. And what was she doing bringing up his penchant for being photographed with a new woman every other week? Oh, why couldn't he just take no for an answer and leave?

"Well, now." His accent slipped into pure Bostonian. "All my bimbos know I'm wicked busy. They tell me I'm worth the wait."

His grin was so cocky, she couldn't tell if he was reciprocating for her nastiness, or if he was simply speaking the truth. In case it was the truth, she wasn't going to apologize. He had already proven he wouldn't be ignored and when he turned to continue his inspection of the space she knew he wouldn't be going anywhere until he was good and ready. She'd just have to wait him out.

"Fine," she said peevishly after a moment's hesitation. She'd take his bid, and find someone else to do the work.

Chapter Seven

Finn followed Cara throughout the large ground floor space, scribbling notes in a small notepad. Considering her sudden return after such a lengthy absence from Palmerton, and the comprehensive changes she planned for the building, she was serious about making a home here.

He'd be wasting his time trying to romance the building out from under her. The bookstore was lost to him, and he considered that a damn shame. But beyond his desire to own the one hundred year old landmark, he longed to see it restored to its full potential, and the idea of breaking through Cara's protective shell was an itch he couldn't help scratching. The renovations she wanted would offer him an opportunity to do both.

With her tacit approval, he plied her with questions. They discussed the front bank of windows and he agreed her purchase of shutters would go a long way toward battling the temperature issue. The installation of three ceiling fans would do the rest of the job.

He hid a satisfied smile at her coo of delight when he peeled back a corner of the carpet to get a peek at the wood floor beneath. Her idea of installing several windows along the back wall was interesting, though the stairwell leading to the second floor would be a problem. After considering the brick expanse for several minutes, he stood with his hands on his hips.

"It's a load bearing wall. You'd need several beams, cutting down on the amount of space you can utilize. You won't get the kind of natural light you're talking about with only the one section of windows that would allow."

"It'll have to do." She studied the section of wall in question and sighed. "The stairwell takes up most of the wall."

Turning away from her disappointed frown, he contemplated the stairwell silently for several moments, and then began to measure again. The tape measure snaked back into its case with a snick.

"There's another option. You could knock out the existing stairwell and put in a spiral staircase. They're not all that practical for heavy traffic, but since you'll only be using it for personal use, it would work. Especially if you choose a style complementing the age and charm of the building. The structural change would free up all but a corner, giving you a larger portion of the wall for windows."

"Oh, Finn." Excitement brightened her eyes. "Do you really think it could be done?"

He nodded. "It will be tricky, but yeah."

"A spiral staircase." She sighed, the sound wistful.

"I know a guy who custom designs them. I saw one of his finished products in a loft downtown. It's a work of art."

She snorted even as her eyes twinkled with humor. "I'm already sold on the idea, Finnegan. In case you hadn't noticed."

He chuckled and shy color crept over her cheeks.

Ducking her head, she turned to scrutinize the wall. "You said you'd have to work around the beams, how much window space can be gained?"

"We should be able to get three good sized windows in."

She spun back. "Floor to ceiling?"

He smiled at her eager expression. "If that's what you want." He cocked his head and raised an inquisitive brow. "Floor to ceiling?"

She laughed, a sound of pure pleasure, and reached for his hand. "Come here." She pulled him along to the back door, jerking it open to step outside.

He knew the instant she realized what she had done. Her flustered gaze jerked to his amused one, and she let go of his hand as if it scalded. Turning her back on him, she pointed at the expanse of lush, grassy bank sloping down to a fast running creek. The picturesque brook disappeared beneath an old stone bridge. Tall maples and birch crowded the opposite bank.

"That's why I want the windows." Her voice quivered with nerves. "I want to be able to look up when I'm working and see that."

He was grateful she couldn't see his dark and sultry smile. She insisted on keeping as much distance as possible between them, but as she got caught up in the renovation plans, she let down her guard. Whatever her reasons for keeping him at arm's length, she'd forgotten all about them in her excitement over the renovation. Her body relaxed more and more as they moved through the studio together.

She even referred to him by the shortened version of his name, and he liked the soft way she said it. Always before it had been Finnegan, and for the most part, his name sounded like a derogatory term on her lips. No doubt she would try to retrench once she had time to think. Too bad for her he wasn't going to give her that time.

She wasn't relaxed now. Her returned tension showed in the stiff line of her body. A rush of anticipation flooded him as he considered just how he would go about relieving her of her tension. He closed the small distance between them, standing behind her with his mouth a breath from her ear.

"Beautiful." He ignored the tree lined view. The picturesque New England scene couldn't hold a candle to Cara O'Shea.

She shot a glance over her shoulder and he was pleased to see the blush staining her cheeks. Lowering her lashes, she started to move away. He stopped her with a palm to her cheek, and ducking his head, settled his mouth on hers.

She froze as his lips took a slow journey over her wide mouth. He nibbled and teased, and when she didn't pull away, he used his advantage of height and bulk to turn her until she was wrapped in his arms. Only when he held her pressed full against him did he deepen the play of his mouth. He nipped at her full bottom lip, and her soft gasp of surprise sent a lash of heat straight to his groin. He hardened in an instant, slipping his tongue between her parted lips to rub and caress hers, silently demanding her response.

****

She opened her mouth to his exploration, stunned to discover a kiss could be so...well, erotic. Evan's kisses had been soft and gentle, and the few times the boys in high school and college had cornered her to steal a kiss, she'd been frightened or disgusted, or both. She wasn't disgusted now and she couldn't be frightened, not when the heat of his kiss raced through her system like a lit fuse.

With her hands trapped between them, she shivered in delight at the sculpted muscle under her flexing fingertips. He was so big, so warm and solid. Even in the most shocking imaginings she had spun around Palmerton's famous football hero over the years, she'd never come close to the reality of being held tight against his hard body.

Her bones were melting. Could bones melt? Oh, who cared? He shifted his head to take the kiss deeper, and her arms slipped up over those muscled shoulders to shove into his thick hair. A little whimper gurgled in her throat. Oh, yes. Bones *could* melt, if Finn the Fine was the one doing the kissing.

Finn the Fine.

The childhood nickname echoed through her head, and took care of her melting bones. They solidified in a rush. She went poker stiff in his arms, yanking her fingers from his hair and shoving hard against his chest. He released her immediately.

She staggered back several steps. Blinking at the ruddy color staining his cheeks, her heart pounded with panic. "This is exactly why I don't want to hire you."

He jammed one big hand through his hair, the action full of agitation, or irritation, she wasn't sure which. His drawn out sigh sounded weary.

"It was a simple kiss, Cara."

As far as she was concerned, there had been nothing simple about that kiss, and it scared the hell out of her. She'd spent her teenage years idolizing his bigger-than-life persona, and she'd been wrong. It was frightening to find, while her mind placed him firmly in the "off-limits due to character flaws" category, her body didn't seem to give a damn.

"I told you once before." Her voice was both raw and breathy. She cleared her throat. "I'm not interested."

His brow arched dubiously, and when he spoke, the gentleness of his tone did nothing to ease the sting of his words.

"You're interested, all right. You just don't want to be. And you're scared. Because you kissed me back or because you enjoyed it?"

Her chest heaved on a stifled gasp, and she stalked by him to march back inside. He followed, stopping several feet away to watch her digging through a crate at the front of the room.

"Cara, talk to me."

"I'm not scared." She straightened, but refused to meet his probing gaze. Pulling a case of supplies from the crate, she started passed him. He stopped her with a gentle hand on her arm.

"Yes, you are. The question is, why?" His thumb rubbed soothingly across the bare flesh of her upper arm. "I wouldn't hurt you, Cara. I've never hurt a woman in my life."

Her head snapped in his direction. "Tell that to your *wife*." She yanked her arm free and moved behind the counter to begin shoving things onto shelves.

"Ex-wife," he corrected.

"Whatever!"

He stood with his hands on his hips, confusion slipping into his expression. "What, exactly, does my ex-wife have to do with this?"

She slapped a box of brushes on the counter with a thump, leaning forward to give him a steady glare. She didn't answer him directly, saying instead, "There's physical hurt, and then there's emotional hurt."

"You're obviously accusing me of one of those. Which is it?" His deep voice told of his rising annoyance, going cold and clipped.

"I've personally experienced the kind of hurt infidelity can cause."

Stunned disbelief skittered across his features. "You think I cheated on Andrea?"

She really didn't want to have this conversation, but maybe it was best she put her cards on the table, so to speak. Sometime in the past half hour, she'd decided she wanted Finn to do the work on her studio. What she *didn't* want were personal complications.

She'd told him she wasn't interested. He simply didn't believe her, and considering her reaction to that bone-melting kiss, why would he? But he would, once he understood the depth of her disdain. She leaned back against the counter and crossed her arms.

"I seem to recall seeing you a couple of years back, having dinner with a very attractive blonde. Funny, she didn't look anything like your wife."

For several heartbeats his face went completely blank, then disappointed resentment hardened his eyes. He raked them over her as if he were looking at something distasteful. When he finally spoke, his voice dripped sarcasm.

"No, she didn't, did she? She didn't appear anything like a high-powered divorce attorney, either. But she sure as hell acted like one, when my loving wife decided she didn't like the idea of being married to a washed up jock after my second knee surgery." His furious gaze seared her uneasy one. "Get your facts straight before you accuse, O'Shea."

For such a big man, he moved quickly. He stalked across the room to wrench open the door. Fury blazed from his eyes when he paused to glance back.

"Ralph Gillespie can take care of the changes you want made to the building. I'll tell him to give you a call."

She winced at the crash of the slamming door.

Well, crap.

She didn't even consider he'd been lying. No one was that good an actor. Okay, so she'd jumped to the wrong conclusion, but everyone in town knew of her father's infidelity. Considering her experience with Tom, could Finn really blame her for faulty assumptions?

Of course he could, and did.

As much as she hated the idea, she'd have to apologize. Not right away, though. Not while he was so angry. The fury in his eyes was hot enough to singe, but the accompanying flash of disappointment was to blame for the guilt squeezing her heart.

She still didn't want a personal entanglement with him, even if he hadn't turned out to be a cheating dog as she assumed. He'd hit the nail on the head when he said she was scared. More like terrified. The way she burned at his touch proved she had no defense against him, and though she was no longer a shy teenager, Michael Finnegan was way out of her league.

He said to get her facts straight, before he effectively withdrew his offer of a bid. Well, she didn't want Ralph Gillespie, whoever he was, tearing into her studio. She wanted Finn. He'd do it right.

As he had moved throughout the bottom floor of her new home, it became evident he loved the old building as much as she did, and was proud of the work he'd already done. She'd use that possessive streak to get him to change his mind. And she'd get her facts straight, before she offered an apology.

She'd talk to Maive.

Chapter Eight

Cara entered through the back door of the house where she'd grown up. "Ma? Is anybody home?"

"I'm in the den."

Grabbing a soda from the fridge, Cara walked through the silent house. She found Mary with her feet up on the coffee table. A box of old pictures sat on the floor beside her and a pile of photographs rested in her lap.

"What are you doing?" Clearing a space beside her, Cara sat down and picked up a stack of photos. She grinned at the discolored picture of her and her sisters from years earlier, grinning like maniacs while sitting astride matching bicycles in front of a Christmas tree.

"I'm sorting through these old shots. I thought Erin would like to have the ones of her, now that she's married."

Cara leaned over to peer at the picture on top of the pile Mary held. Erin, in her high school cheering uniform, preened for the camera. Cara laughed. "She always was a ham."

Mary smiled. "She never had a shy bone in her body, that's for sure."

"Unlike some of us," Cara grumbled in good-natured acceptance.

"There's something to be said for being a little

timid on occasion." Mary bumped her shoulder into Cara's in a gentle nudge. "You always studied the situation before jumping in with both feet. It saved you from being sorry later, like your sister often was, on more than one occasion."

"And kept me from *experiencing the moment*, according to Erin."

"I recall a number of times when I could have wished you hadn't experienced the moment quite so enthusiastically," Mary scolded with a laugh. "Like the time you slipped the waxed paper under Aunt Paula's backside on the park slide."

Cara burst out laughing. Aunt Paula had shot down the slide like a bullet. She'd landed in the dirt six feet away and had to sit on a pillow for the rest of her visit. Cara had been grounded for a week.

She snickered. "I can still see her face."

Mary's smile was reluctant. "It was an awful thing to do."

"I know, but who knew it would work so well? We saved our money to buy our own waxed paper after that. We charged a nickel a sheet and made a dollar-fifty profit off the neighborhood kids."

"Sometimes I'm glad I didn't know everything you girls were up to. I'd have been gray at thirty."

Mary paused in sorting the photos when she came across a picture of her and Tom, smiling at the camera on a beach with a brilliant sunset in the background.

"Ma." Cara draped an arm around her shoulders.

Mary tossed the picture on to the growing pile, and shook her head. "I'm fine. I was just remembering how much fun we all had on that trip."

"Come on, Ma."

At Cara's doubtful tone, Mary set the pile of pictures on the table. "Honestly, Cara. You don't need to look at me like I'm going to shatter."

"I worry about you, Ma. What he did to you was so unfair."

Mary dropped her head to Cara's shoulder for just a moment. "I know you worry, but you don't have to." She straightened and brushed the hair back from Cara's face. "It's been a long time, sweetheart. Believe it or not, I'm happy with my life, and your father and I have come to a workable understanding."

She knew they had. She just didn't understand it and didn't think she ever would. "He wants to talk to me. He's left several messages on my machine."

"And what do you want?"

"I don't know, Ma." She stood, too agitated to sit, and began to pace. "I don't know what he expects me to say to him, and I can't think what he could possibly have to say to me."

"Maybe he wants to tell you he loves you."

"God." Instant tears clouded her vision. She swiped at them with stiff fingers. "How can you defend him?"

"I'm not."

"Please," Cara huffed, and shook her head in disbelief.

"Don't take that tone with me, Cara Brennan," Mary said sharply, her mouth stretched tight in a disapproving line.

"I'm sorry. I'm sorry, Ma." Returning home was proving more difficult than she'd imagined. So many conflicting emotions swirling just beneath the surface left her floundering. She lost the battle with her tears, but tried to laugh them off with a weak smile. Her mother wasn't buying it. She rose from the couch and wrapped Cara in her gentle arms.

"Sweetheart, I know he hurt and disappointed you in the worst way possible. He hurt and disappointed me, too, and for a long time I struggled to forgive him. But over time, I've come to understand what he did, which he didn't do maliciously. He loves you girls so much, and it pains him to know how much he's hurt you."

Cara pulled back and swiped at her nose with the back of her hand. "Am I supposed to feel sorry for him because he's hurting? He made his choices and to hell with all of us."

"No, sweetheart. No one expects you to feel sorry for him. You're entitled to feel however you feel, but look at you. The situation with your father is tearing you apart because you've never really dealt with it. Wouldn't you feel better if you understood his reasons? Knowledge is power, as they say."

"I'll never understand him," Cara sniffed.

"Not if you never try." Mary held up a hand when Cara opened her mouth to object. "If you don't want to talk to him, that's your choice. But isn't that how you've handled the situation so far? It doesn't appear to have made you very happy. I want my babies to be happy."

Mary pulled a tissue from her pocket. Cara accepted it and blew her nose.

"Did you know your father knew Hannah before we were married?"

Cara froze with the tissue pressed to her nose. "What?"

"They dated in high school."

"Does that make what they did right?" Cara

demanded. How could her mother be so accepting? She was talking about her husband, who had left her for another woman.

"No, it doesn't make anything right," Mary answered softly. "But time moves on. I've gotten over it. Can you say the same?" When Cara remained silent, Mary sighed. "This estrangement between the two of you has left you sad. I'm afraid it's going to make you bitter." She tucked an errant curl behind Cara's ear. "I know a good portion of the anger you have for your father is on my behalf."

"And justified," Cara insisted.

"Yes, it's justified, but I don't *want* that responsibility, Cara. I don't want to be responsible for you not having a father, even an imperfect one. What's between Tom and me is our business. If you want to be mad at him for something he did to you, fine, that's your right. I just can't stand the idea of you cutting yourself off from him as a kind of backhanded support for me."

She patted Cara's cheek and returned to the sofa. "You haven't yet learned the truth of this apparently, but nobody's perfect, sweetheart. I'm not being glib," she insisted when Cara rolled her eyes. "What I'm trying to say is, everyone has something about them that you won't like, even those you love the most. If you shove everyone who ever disappoints you out of your life, you're going to end up a lonely hermit."

Guilty as charged. Since Cara didn't know how to respond, she remained silent.

"Talk to him, Cara. It's up to you whether you can forgive him or not once you do. I hate seeing you so miserable, and until you settle things with your father, well...I hate seeing you miserable."

****

The idea of talking to her father made Cara's stomach ache, so she put it out of her mind. As it turned out, her talk with *Maive* also had to wait. Which was just as well. If the curt nod Finn gave Cara two days later, when he passed her at the permit counter in the town hall, was any indication, he would need more time to get over his anger.

She'd decided to go ahead and get the permit paperwork for the renovation started, even before they'd settled things—*if* things between them *could* be settled. She was itching to get started, and Maive's unexpected absence, while visiting her great grandchildren for a few days, only added to the delay. Cara hadn't had a chance to talk to Finn's great aunt yet, and she wasn't going to go begging for forgiveness until she had.

On Saturday morning, she walked the two blocks to the Palmer House Restaurant to meet Erin, just back from her honeymoon. Strolling along the tree-lined sidewalk, Cara dodged two young boys on skateboards. She grinned at the rhythmic clatter of the hard rubber wheels calling out a steady cadence on the seamed cement pathway.

Her eyes drank in the familiar sights of the various homes and storefronts of the town center. With the exception of the new library across from the town hall, built a few years back, and the bright neon sign flashing outside the video store where Pandy's market used to be, she could be thirteen again, racing to meet Meggy for an ice cream at the Dairy Barn.

She chuckled at the memory.

Thinking of Meggy, she considered her reason for meeting Erin this morning. A sous chef at one of the more upscale restaurants in Boston, Meggy had long dreamed of running her own kitchen. Her eyes lit with interest yesterday when Jill Carlson, who it appeared was the current president of the town grapevine, had stopped by the studio to announce the historic Palmer House restaurant might soon be on the market. Jill breezed out of the studio after a twenty-minute gossip session, and Cara immediately turned to her friend.

"Are you interested in buying the restaurant?"

"Are you kidding me? The property is gorgeous. And this close to Boston, it's a prime location. Close enough to draw people from the city, without the overhead of a downtown location. With the right menu..." Meggy sighed wistfully, shaking her head. "But I could never swing it. I have some money put aside, but not nearly enough. I'm not ready yet. Besides, I'm a chef, not a businesswoman. What the hell do I know about running a restaurant? I wouldn't know where to begin on the business side."

The germ of an idea sprouted in Cara's mind. "Shan's been managing Spinelli's for six years."

Meggy's brows jumped together in interest. "Do you think she'd be interested? Does she have any money?"

"I have no idea if she'd be interested, and I doubt she has any money." The cautious excitement in Meggy's eyes faded. "I, on the other hand, do have money." Cara grinned.

She had cautioned Meggy that Shan may not be interested regardless, and decided to check with Mrs. Hawkins before she approached her sister with the idea.

Years of sampling Meggy's and Shan's recipes convinced Cara the two women would cook circles around the short order cook at the family restaurant. However, if the owner wasn't considering selling, there would be no point in pursuing the idea.

Erin waited at the front counter, flashing her wedding band at the teenage hostess when Cara arrived at the Palmer House.

"Erin, Erin, married lady."

"Cara!" Erin spun around and grabbed Cara in a hug.

"How was the honeymoon?" She laughed when her vivacious sister fanned her face with her hand while rolling her eyes to the back of her head. "That bad, huh? Do we need to have a family meeting, so I can explain the birds and the bees to my new brother-in-law?"

Erin's smile was dreamy. "Oh, Cara. It was so beautiful. Bermuda is another world!"

"So I've heard." She glanced at the teenage hostess. "We need a table, please." When they were seated, Cara grinned. "Well, marriage certainly agrees with you. You look like a million bucks."

"I feel like a billion!" They gave their orders to the waitress, and Erin leaned forward on her elbows. "So, how's the studio coming along?"

"The plans are made and the permits have been filed. I'm just waiting on the contractor." She was hedging, but Finn and that disaster in her studio the other day weren't something she planned to discuss, with anyone.

When Mrs. Hawkins exited the kitchen, she immediately ambled over to their table. She smiled down at Erin. "If it isn't Mrs. Espizitto!"

Erin beamed a delighted smile. "Hello, Mrs. Hawkins. Do you remember my sister, Cara?"

"Of course I do. I hear welcome home is in order."

"Yes, it is." Cara returned the older woman's smile.

"I also heard you bought the old book store. That must have made Finn crazy! He's been after Maive to sell it to him for years."

Cara blinked. She'd forgotten how few secrets there were in Palmerton. "He'll get over it." She bared her teeth in a sly grin and Mrs. Hawkins laughed. "There's another interesting bit of gossip going around town," Cara introduced. "Rumor is you want to retire to spend more time with your grandkids."

If Mrs. Hawkins was surprised people knew her private business, she didn't show it. She smiled serenely, and nodded. "I've been in business for twenty-six years. It's time I remove my apron and take my grandbabies to Disneyworld."

"Have you had any offers on the place?" Cara ignored the questioning stare Erin shot at her.

"As I haven't actually put it on the market yet, no, I haven't. Why? I thought you were an artist not a restaurateur."

Cara laughed. "Oh, painting is my forte. The only thing I know how to do with food is eat it."

Mrs. Hawkins chuckled and moved aside when the waitress appeared with their breakfasts. "Well then, I'll leave you to enjoy your meals."

"What was that all about?" Erin asked the moment Mrs. Hawkins walked away.

Cara salted her omelet. "How do you think Shan

would feel about becoming the owner of her own restaurant?"

Erin leaned back in her chair. "Are you serious?"

"I don't know. That depends on Shan, and Meggy. Between the two of them they could give the other three restaurants in town a run for their money, don't you think?"

Erin tapped her fork on the table, as if considering the idea. "I think Shan would love it, but you know she'll balk at the idea of you lending her the money."

Cara shrugged. "Maybe not. Meggy has some money put aside. She's interested in a partnership with Shan. With Meggy putting up half the money, Shan could consider me a silent investor. It really depends on what Mrs. Hawkins wants for the place."

Erin scooted back her chair. "Let's go ask Shan."

Cara pointed her fork at Erin's full plate. "There's no rush. Eat your breakfast, Mrs. Espizitto."

Chapter Nine

Shan balked at the idea, just as Erin predicted, but her eyes were full of the same cautious excitement Cara had seen in Meggy's. And Cara knew her sister. The seed was planted. Shan would mull it over. All Cara had to do was sit back and let her.

For what seemed like the millionth time, she sent a silent thanks to Evan Malone. His friendship eased the loneliness during her eight years of self-exile, and his belief in her as an artist had brought her success beyond her dreams.

The memory of his grin the day he handed her that first, stunning commission check made her laugh aloud. God, she loved having a healthy bank account! Give her a beard and a belly and she'd give Santa a run for his money.

A wide smile tipped her lips as she rang Maive's doorbell.

"You look like the cat that swallowed the canary." Maive pushed open door. "Did you find a lost Rembrandt behind a wall in that building you stole from me?"

Cara laughed and followed her into the parlor. Maive moved to an open curio cabinet and resumed dusting the delicate figurines filling every shelf.

"I didn't steal a thing from you, if I can believe my

accountant. It sent him into convulsions having to write you that check."

Maive harrumphed and swiped at a porcelain southern belle with the feather duster in her hand.

"Your carpenter may disagree with that opinion though. The stealing part." Cara ran her fingers over the back of the settee. "He seems pretty possessive of my new home."

"It's not good for a man to always get everything he wants." Maive waived the duster dismissively. "Disappointment builds character. Missing out on the place will be good for the boy."

"And you think Michael Finnegan needs his character built?"

Maive turned, studying her. "I didn't say that. Finn's as fine a man as they come. He's just led a charmed life. That kind of thing can make a man overconfident."

"He is that," Cara complained beneath her breath.

"So, you've come to talk about Finn." Maive lowered to her favorite seat and waved for Cara to sit. "You won't find a more talented craftsman in this county."

"His talent as a carpenter isn't in question."

When Cara fell silent, Maive scowled at her. "Spit it out, girl. I'm ninety years old. I could keel over before you say what's on your mind."

Cara choked on a laugh, though she needed to tread lightly. The old lady was too perceptive for her own good, and Cara had never been very adept at concealing her emotions when it came to Finn. To avoid blurting out the entire embarrassing incident at the studio the other day, she asked, "Has he always gotten everything he wanted?"

"What kind of idiotic question is that?" Maive snorted. "You want me to answer your questions, you ask me straight out. What is it you want to know?"

Swallowing nerves threatening to choke her, Cara inhaled a deep breath. "I want to know about Andrea."

"You want to know about his ex-wife?" Maive eyes glittered with speculation.

"It's not what you think," Cara quickly added.

"And just what is it I'm thinking?"

She was digging a hole deeper every time she opened her mouth. In the interest of self-preservation, she got to the point. "Finn told me Andrea left him because he retired from football."

Maive nodded and her eyes went hard. "The woman was and is an insatiable social climber. I never knew what the boy saw in her. She loved the idea of being the wife of a famous quarterback infinitely more than she ever loved him—if she loved him at all. She married a congressman from Pennsylvania three months after the divorce. Good riddance, I say."

Hearing his claim validated, a knot of guilt tighten in Cara's stomach. Not that she'd actually doubted him. She simply found it hard to believe any woman would walk away from a man like Finn of her own accord. Apparently Andrea the Addlepated had done just that— and assigning ridiculous appellations to a woman she never even met was a sure sign she was losing her mind.

She realized she'd been staring into space for too long when Maive purred, "So, our Finn told you about his ex-wife, did he?"

Too rattled to be evasive, Cara muttered miserably.

"I sort of asked him about her." When Maive didn't prod further, only sat there grinning, Cara rolled her eyes and explained. "Actually, I...sort of accused him of being unfaithful to her."

Maive's gray brows snapped together, all hint of amusement gone. "The hell you say! My boy would never do any such thing."

"I know that...now." Cara squeezed her hands together on her lap.

"What were you thinking? Accusing him of something like that?"

"I had my reasons." Her defense sounded weak, even to her own ears. When Maive continued to frown, she blinked guiltily. "Okay, so I was wrong. I'm going to apologize, but he's so angry with me he's refusing to do the work on the studio. He told me to call some guy named Gillespie."

"Of course he's angry. I'd have been shocked if he wasn't." Maive leaned back on the settee. "His divorce is a sore spot for him. It's the one time in his life he failed, and failed big in his mind."

Cara grimaced and bit her lower lip. "You're not making me feel any better."

"Was I supposed to?"

She closed her eyes at the caustic reply and flopped back in the chair, defeated.

"Why would you accuse him of something like that, anyway? Do you even know Andrea?"

She opened her eyes and met Maive's steady gaze, unsure what to say. She wasn't sure she could explain, even if she wanted to. "It's a long story."

"And an even longer history?" Maive observed keenly.

Far too perceptive, Cara decided. When she remained stubbornly silent, Maive sighed.

"Not all marriages end due to infidelity, Cara. Some just end. Finn's was one of those, and he was better off when it did." Maive shrugged her thin shoulders before adding, "I happen to know Finn is up at that old rat trap of a place he's restoring this afternoon. You remember where Maple Street is?" She didn't wait for Cara's reply. "It's the old Sawyer place at the end of the street. You can't miss it."

"I'm not sure he'll accept my apology. He was pretty mad."

"Do you want Gillespie doing the renovations on your studio?"

"No. No, I don't."

"Neither does Finn." Maive cackled and sat forward on the settee. "Oh, if I know my boy, he'll make you sweat a little, but he's not going to let that clod Gillespie get his hands on your studio. You owe Finn a genuine apology." Her eyes flashed with mischief. "Once you've given it, offer him the job again. When he refuses, and he will, thank him very sweetly for Gillespie's name. You watch how fast the boy changes his tune."

Cara's lips formed a small smile. It faded quickly. "Why are you helping me? What I accused him of was rotten. I wouldn't help me."

"You'll make it right with him." Maive nodded with firm resolve. "And if I had to guess, I'd say you probably had a good reason for believing something like that of him, even if you turned out to be wrong. Besides..." She settled back once again. "I've seen the way Finn looks at you. I think you'll be good for the boy."

Cara scrambled to her feet. "That's not what I want."

"Isn't it?" Maive studied her with keen eyes. "I've seen the way you look at him, too, girl. The sparks practically fly." She cackled a laugh and rose to link her arm with Cara's, leading her to the front door. "He's just a man, Cara, albeit a fine looking one. Nothing to be scared of." She opened the door and gave Cara a gentle shove onto the porch. "Relax and enjoy the ride, girl. And call me if you mess things up again."

Chapter Ten

Relax and enjoy the ride? Cara was so nervous, she'd be lucky if she made it to the end of Maple Street without plowing into one of the trees lining the quiet road. Maive noticed the way she looked at Finn? Had anyone else? Had Finn? God, she hoped not. Regardless, it didn't matter. She wouldn't be doing anything about the mutual interest obvious to a too perceptive old lady, if no one else.

Cara could measure her knowledge of romantic endeavors in a teacup, while Finn could fill an Olympic swimming pool with his experience with women. A man that skilled in romance would rip her to shreds, and whistle a happy tune as he walked away.

Considering his reputation, she was ten kinds of a fool to even consider signing him on to renovate her studio. But apparently she was okay with being a fool, because here she was, climbing the wide steps to the old Sawyer estate. She passed between the towering white columns of the one hundred-and-ten-year-old Georgian Revival, and pressed her finger to the doorbell.

A fresh coat of paint made the spooky mausoleum she remembered shine like a well-loved home. The glossy, eight-foot oak door gleamed like a large wooden portal, beckoning visitors to come inside and rest.

As she waited, she tugged nervously at her light-weight peach sweater, smoothing it over the waist of her short denim skirt. Her heart pounded erratically in her chest. She shouldn't have worn this outfit, it was too girly, and she shouldn't have worn her power heels, but the strappy, white Prada sandals said *I'm a woman of confidence*. And right now, she needed all the confidence she could muster.

When all remained quiet inside the old house, she heaved a sigh of relief, and turned to leave, happy to put off her apology for another time. The door swinging wide crushed her newly hatched relief and left her staring into Finn's cool, blue eyes.

Oh yeah, he's still mad as hell.

Before she could chicken out, she plunged into the apology she owed him. "I'm sorry, Finn. I made an assumption and...I'm sorry."

He stood silently, a blank expression on his face while his eyes studied her. The moment stretched out until she decided he could stick her sincere apology in any orifice he chose. She was about to suggest just that, when he swung the door wide.

"Come on in," he invited grudgingly.

She moved passed him and her eyes widened at the truly incredible staircase at the end of the grand foyer. The eight-foot wide flight leading to the second story curved majestically, the intricate carvings of the banister continuing all the way to the top to run along the hallway to the second floor rooms.

The door clicked shut behind her, and she whirled to face him. Swallowing, she held out the six pack of beer she picked up on her way.

"A peace offering."

He took the package from her hand, and motioned for her to follow, guiding her down a long corridor to the left of the staircase.

"Oh." She inhaled an admiring gasp as he pushed open a swinging wooden panel, and she stepped into a huge, homey kitchen. Her eyes roamed over the custom cabinets, the wide plank wooden floor, and finally, the built-in breakfast nook below a large bay window.

"This is gorgeous, Finn." He grunted and pulled two beers from the box, holding one out to her. She shook her head. "I don't drink beer."

His eyes narrowed. "You drank wine at the wedding. What's the matter? Is beer too common for a famous artist like yourself?"

Definitely still mad.

Well, she'd accused him of something pretty nasty. He was entitled to a little retribution. She'd allow him a swipe or two.

"No." Ignoring his sneer, she glanced around the beautiful kitchen. "I just don't metabolize beer very well." He'd never know how true that was. She had learned the hard way on a cool June night years ago.

He replaced the bottle in the empty slot with a shrug. "Would you like a tour?"

"I think I would. Thank you."

"This is the kitchen."

His sharp tone told her he hadn't expected her to accept, and wasn't happy she had. Too bad. She didn't mind throwing him a few curves while he got in his swipes.

"It's beautiful." The rich wood of the cabinetry reminded her of the built-in shelving in the bookstore.

She smiled, recognizing his work. "Did you do the woodwork in here?"

"I've done all the renovation around here," he said in a clipped tone.

He marched ahead of her, hurrying her through the sixteen room, seventy-five hundred square-foot home. Most of the renovation was finished from what she could see. Only two of the six bedrooms on the second floor still had the neglected appearance she expected to find throughout the house, considering how long the place had been vacant.

The seven fireplaces throughout the home were each more impressive than the last, the mantels amazing. He said the spiral staircase he'd seen was a work of art, but he was an artist himself.

He grunted noncommittally when she told him so. Did he think she was using flattery to soften him up so he'd accept her apology? She shrugged inwardly. That was fine with her. It allowed her to praise him in a way she would have been reluctant to do under normal circumstances. The warm, stunning showcase of a home he had created reinforced her belief he should do the work in her studio.

To that end, she took Maive's advice when he ended the tour a few short minutes later, staring at her like a not-so-polite stranger at the open front door.

"I wish you'd reconsider taking on the work I need done at the studio. You've done beautiful work here, Finn. I want the same attention to detail for my own home."

Hard blue eyes pinned her to the spot. "Gillespie is a harmless grandfather and a passable carpenter. He'll give you what you want without making you freeze up like a frightened little girl."

The insult stung like a cold slap. Wow! That hurt. Okay, she'd just given him his last damn swipe.

The bastard.

She met his angry gaze with the lift of her chin. "Maybe you're right." She turned away and walked out onto the porch before she gave in to the urge to belt him. "Thanks for the tour, Finnegan."

She was half way down the steps when he growled. "I'll be there at eight on Monday morning."

She wished she could laugh at his capitulation—her esteem for Maive's predictive abilities shooting up several points—but she was still smarting from his cutting remark. So, instead of grinning and claiming victory, she kept right on walking, without looking back.

"I'll expect you at seven. Don't be late."

****

The three inch heels of her sexy sandals clacked against the flagstone walkway like rifle shots, but her angry stride did nothing to mar the seductive view. Above the mile of tanned, gut-wrenching legs, her shapely ass swished beneath the denim excuse for a skirt she wore. He frowned, unable to tear his gaze away until she climbed into her vehicle. The woman was driving him crazy.

Uttering a raw curse, he slammed the door with a thud. She had placed him in the same cheating husband category as her father, and though he understood how she could have come to that conclusion, he didn't deserve her disdain.

When she threw her infuriating accusation in his face, it had been all he could do not to shake her, he'd been so angry. He'd been faithful to Andrea, damn it, even when their long-troubled marriage started to go to shit.

His ex-wife's calm announcement, that he had lost his appeal once his pro career ended, ripped at his pride, leaving what little was left in tatters. The memory still had the ability to make him fume.

He spent the last four years burning his way through a series of utterly forgettable women, proving his ex-wife wrong, but the victory had been hollow. When it came to women, he'd been living life in the fast lane. Hell, more like the sexual equivalent of the autobahn. After racing down that road for so long, he red-lined, and finally, spun out.

Ultimately, none of the women, no matter how beautiful, were able to heal the shards of desperation piercing his soul. His failure to hold Andrea's interest was always at the back of his mind, and none of the beauties sharing his bed had been important enough to allow him to overcome his failure. After four years, he'd lost all interest in trying.

His physical awareness of Cara O'Shea was the first tickle of real attraction he had experienced for a woman in months, and she seemed to be the only person on the planet who didn't know the facts surrounding his divorce.

Well, she knew now. The question was, would it make any difference? She'd said she wasn't interested, when the truth of the matter was, she didn't want to be. Because she thought he was like her father? Would that change now that she knew the truth, or was there some other reason for her apprehension whenever he was around?

Instant guilt had slashed through him at the hurt flashing in her eyes when he blasted her with that frightened little girl insult, but she'd pissed him off, damn it. And a frightened little girl was exactly what she resembled when she ran back inside her studio.

He all but imploded during that heated embrace, despite it being obvious she didn't have a clue what she was doing in the kissing department. How the hell did a woman who looked the way she did have little to no experience kissing a man? Despite her bunny-of-the-month body, the average high school girl had more experience than Cara O'Shea.

Not that her lack of knowledge mattered a bit at the time. The moment he held her flush against him, his mind ceased to function. If she hadn't gone stiff in his arms, he didn't know what would have happened. Dragging her down onto the lawn and not letting her up until they both lost all reason, and found paradise, had been a distinct possibility considering the way he'd been feeling...until she turned into a spitting cat.

When he broke the kiss and stared into her eyes, he found anger there, anger that didn't quite conceal the same fear he'd seen in her expressive eyes several times before.

If she hadn't been responding to him, he would have understood her reaction. Having a man's tongue halfway down your throat would be alarming to a woman who kissed like a twelve year-old. But he had held enough women to know when one was fully engaged, and Cara O'Shea had been more than engaged. She burned like a flame in his arms. His nerve endings were seared wherever their bodies touched.

It didn't make sense. She didn't make sense. The

woman was a puzzle, and dammed if he wasn't itching to get his hands on the pieces again.

Suddenly, Monday morning couldn't come soon enough.

Chapter Eleven

A heavy knocking rattled Cara's door at seven-o-five Monday morning. Five cups of coffee and three dozen donuts were shoved into her hands the moment the door opened and Finn, followed by Ryan, and two men she had never met, filed inside.

Ryan swept her into a hug, forcing her to juggle the coffee before she scalded one or both of them. Plucking one of the cups out of the box, he grinned.

"Finn decided he needed a little slave labor to get those shelves out of here this morning. If it had been anyone other than you getting me out of bed this early, when I'm technically still on my honeymoon, my wife would have knocked me over the head with that new rolling pin Meggy gave her as a shower gift."

Cara returned his grin, trying to picture her petite sister wielding the culinary weapon against her six foot groom.

"These other two slaves are Bob and Steve Burns." Finn lifted three cups from where she balanced them in front of her. He handed one to each of the Burns brothers as he made introductions.

His tone of voice was friendly and though he wore that dimpled smile she'd begun to hate, she sighed with relief. She hadn't known what to expect after their last encounter. Apparently he'd decided to put his hostility behind him, or ignore it while they were working together. Either possibility worked for her. It would make the job a lot easier if they weren't snarling at each other constantly.

Cara took the last coffee and opened the first box of donuts on the counter. Two boxes were polished off while the men discussed the best way to remove the shelving without damaging the woodwork or the floor. An hour and a half later, the shelving units were loaded and lashed on a trailer out front. Finn would deliver them to the day camp later.

Cara thanked Bob and Steve for their help before they left, and stood marveling at the amount of space removing the shelves opened up. The room was huge!

She scrambled to help when Finn and Ryan pulled the mounting from the counter cabinet and maneuvered it to the center of the room. She had decided to keep it to use as a wet bar that would be the focal point of the seating area she envisioned for the front corner.

"Oh, wow!" Dropping to her knees, she ran her hand over the six foot expanse of hardwood flooring exposed.

Finn stood with his hands on his hips beside her.

"Let's pull the carpeting up and see what kind of shape the rest of the floor is in."

"Now?" Sitting back on her heels, she spun her head to stare up at him.

"Did you want to wait?" Amusement was clear in his tone.

"No, I just didn't think…" She scrambled to her feet and dusted her hands on her jeans. "Where do we start?"

Ryan pulled a claw-like tool from a toolbox and

went to the far corner of the room. With an easy tug, he peeled back a section of the carpet, exposing the padding beneath. Finn and Cara spread out along the front of the room, and together, the three of them accomplished the dusty job of rolling the carpeting in sections and removing the padding.

Cara fanned at the dusty cloud floating weightless in the morning sunlight, her eyes on the golden wood they exposed. Other than an occasional dull spot, the floor was in good shape, and beautiful. The smooth wood softened the appearance of the large space, and she loved the contrast of warm wood against the weathered brick of the back wall. She shivered with a secret thrill of ownership. The studio portion of her home would be even more beautiful than she imagined.

"Looks good." Ryan's voice echoed in the empty room, along with the clank of the tools he replaced in his toolbox.

"Good?" Busy angling the newly installed wooden shutters at the front of the room, Cara turned to gawk at him. "It's gorgeous!"

"It will be." Finn spoke in a distracted tone as he studied the back wall.

The front door opening prevented Cara from commenting. She stiffened when she found Tom standing just inside the door. The lengthening silence was deafening as father and daughter stared at each other across the small space.

"Good morning, Tom." Finn's deep voice cut through the tension.

"Finn." Tom nodded a greeting. The smile he offered Ryan was strained. "Hello, Ryan. I hear Erin is already planning the second honeymoon."

Ryan laughed and crossed the floor to shake his new father-in-law's hand. "That works for me, especially if I don't have to do any heavy lifting." He winked at Cara.

She gave him a weak smile. "I appreciate your help this morning."

"Anytime." He hefted the toolbox from the counter and looked at Finn. "Let me know when you're ready to yank the stairwell."

Finn nodded and checked his watch. "We have an appointment to see the spiral stairs in a couple of hours. I'll have a better idea on when we'll be ready after we meet with the manufacturer."

Cara shot Finn a glance. This was the first she'd heard of the appointment, but she wasn't going to look a gift horse in the mouth. She wasn't ready to talk to Daddy, though it seemed he was going to force the issue. She'd take the excuse of meeting with the manufacturer today, even if it meant having to spend time alone with Finn.

Tom waited until Ryan left before turning to her. "We need to talk, Cara."

"Now isn't a good time."

He proved he could be just as stubborn as she. "When is?"

Cara's gaze flicked to Finn, who was watching their little family drama with interest. He stood with his arms crossed, his face expectant, as though he were waiting for her answer himself.

"What time is this appointment?"

He didn't react to her hostile tone, answering easily. "A couple of hours. We should be done by three."

She turned back to Tom. "Since you're obviously not going to let this go, I'll meet you in the park across from your office at four."

She wasn't interested in having the coming confrontation in a restaurant where inquiring ears would surely be tuned in to pick up details for the grapevine, but neither did she want to meet him at his home or office with Hannah present. The park would have to do.

Her stomach muscles clenched at the soft smile spreading over his face.

"Thank you."

"I said I'd meet you," she informed him coolly. "I'm not promising anything else."

His smile dimmed and he lifted his hand toward her face. He quickly dropped his arm to his side when she stiffened. He sighed.

"I'll see you at four, Cara mine. Finn." He offered Finn a smile before leaving.

The moment the door closed behind him, Cara let out a shaky breath, her shoulders slumping. She dropped her head forward and squeezed her eyes shut, rubbing her forehead with stiff fingers.

She didn't hear Finn approach, and flinched when he rested his hands on her shoulders. He stood close behind her. She could actually feel the warmth of his body along her back, and was shocked at how much she wanted to lean against him, to let him hold her for just a few minutes.

But resting in Finn's arms was a luxury she couldn't allow herself. She didn't lean back as she wanted, but she couldn't step away either.

"He did that on purpose," she complained.

"What?" His fingers flexed on her taut shoulder muscles in a gentle massage.

"Came here when he knew I wasn't alone."

"Would you have talked to him if you'd been alone?"

She shifted her shoulders under his hands in a shrug. "I don't know, maybe. Probably not."

She would have to talk to her father eventually, now that she was back. Her mother and sisters had long since come to terms with the situation, and wanted her to as well. She'd try, if only to ease her mother's mind.

"What has you so upset? He's your father, Cara, not a firing squad."

She shot him an annoyed scowl over her shoulder and shrugged out from under his soothing hands. She had no interest in discussing her estrangement with her father. It was uncomfortable enough to think about, never mind share with a man she should be doing her best to avoid.

"It's complicated," she said finally.

"You haven't spoken to him since he married Hannah. That's a long time to go without talking to your father."

She hadn't spoken to Daddy for much longer than that, but Finn's blunt statement made her jaw drop.

"Everyone in town knows you refuse to speak to him." He arched his eyebrows as if to say she shouldn't be surprised her personal business was common knowledge around town.

She shouldn't be, but she was. And the realization made her bitter. "I guess when the town manager leaves his wife and children for another woman, it makes the town grapevine."

He was silent for a moment. "I have some experience with being the topic of gossip around town, around the country for that matter. It's obvious you don't like it any more than I do, and like me, there's nothing you can do about it."

Since he was right, she said nothing.

"He didn't leave you, Cara. He left Mary."

It sure hurt like he'd left her. "Please don't defend him."

"I'm not defending what he did. I'm just stating the facts." She glared at him and he chuckled. "Now that you're mad at me again, instead of stressing over something you've agreed to do anyway, why don't we get going?"

As they pulled away from the curb in his big pick-up, Finn lifted a manila envelope from the seat next to him and dropped it in her lap.

"What's this?"

"My bid." He shrugged a shoulder. "We should be able to do everything you want, and stay within the budget you mentioned."

She slid a fingertip under the fold and pulled out the stack of papers. She read the detailed list of supplies on the top page.

"There are two options in there for the back wall." He glanced her way before returning his attention to the road. "I got to thinking, instead of the windows you want, why not put in a wall of French doors? A couple of doors would give you the light you want, and you have enough level ground off the back of the building to lay out a small patio. You'd have a quiet place to enjoy that view you're so excited about."

She darted a glance at him. If he was trying to

remind her of what happened between them when she showed him that view, he wasn't being blatant about it.

As if she needed to be reminded about that kiss. That kiss hadn't been far from her mind for days.

She studied his strong profile for a moment, before glancing back at the papers in her hand. Oh, she was in big trouble. She'd known working with him would be a huge mistake, and she was right. Here it was only the first day and she already had to fight the overwhelming urge to fall into his arms and accept all he wanted to give her. Her heart would be broken before they were finished, and if that scene in the studio a few minutes earlier were any indication, she wasn't doing a very good job at keeping it from happening.

She concentrated on the papers. Flipping through the pages, she paused when she came to a sketched drawing laying out his vision for the back wall. Her eyebrows rose in silent appreciation. The simple pencil sketch depicted the aged brick of the back wall as a backdrop for an elegantly simple, spiral staircase. To the left of the stairs were three double-hinged wooden doors, open to reveal a cozy seating area, complete with bistro table and chair.

"You drew this?"

She glanced at him and his gaze dropped to the pages she held. He shrugged and turned back to the road. "It helps when I can see the finished look I'm shooting for. There's a sketch in there with windows if you don't like the idea of the doors. Like I said, it's just an option."

"It's a good option. I love it." She flipped to the second sketch, silently appreciating it for its artistic value for several moments. Having already decided on the doors, or nothing, she returned the stack of papers to the envelope. She shook her head. "You keep surprising me, Finnegan."

His gaze tangled with hers. "Why is that, O'Shea?"

"As an artist, I recognize talent when I see it. These sketches…" She tapped a finger to the envelope in her lap. "They're good. Is there anything you can't do?"

Amusement darkened his eyes. "I can't cook."

She snorted a quiet laugh. "Neither can I. That's Meggy's and Shan's department."

"I was just kidding." He grinned. "You can't cook?"

"You can?"

"Of course I can. Everyone can cook."

"I beg to differ." She sniffed to suppress the smile that threatened. "In fact, the last time Meggy came to stay with me in New York, she complained about having to dust the oven before she could use it. Basically, I have a kitchen because one comes with every apartment."

His deep bark of laughter filled the cab of the truck, and she went warm and jittery at the same time.

"I think you're being too hard on yourself, O'Shea. Everyone can cook, even if it's just toasting bread or heating a can of soup."

She snorted dismissively. "If that's what qualifies as cooking in your mind, then maybe you're being too generous with yourself!"

He shrugged unapologetically. "Hey, cooking's cooking."

She bared her teeth in a taunting grin. "I can throw a football. By your standards, that makes me a quarterback."

He shook his head and chuckled, slipping into a thick, Boston accent. "Well, now. Yawh wicked clevah, O'Shea. Explaining things in a way a jauck like me can undastand."

She preened shamelessly, batting her eyelashes. "I try."

"Do you miss it?" he asked several moments later. "Living in New York City?"

She shook her head. "I haven't been home very long yet, but, no. I don't miss it. I miss the friends I made there, but New York was never home. What about you?" She shifted on the seat and bent her leg to fold her ankle under her other knee, facing him more completely. "Do you miss the football life?"

He shot her a quick glance before answering. "Sometimes. I miss the rush of playing in a big game. Football was such a huge part of my life for so long, it was tough to walk away. Ultimately, the decision to retire was made for me. After the second knee surgery, walking at all was my main concern."

"You seem to have recovered. You're still young enough. Do you ever think about going back?"

"I wouldn't be human if I didn't. But even though the surgery was a success, I don't have full range of motion in my left knee and never will. I was lucky enough to have kept my foot in the door on the broadcasting side of the sport."

She nodded, smiling slightly. "I saw your interview during the game last week. You held your own."

His smile turned wolfish. "You watched me, huh?"

She rolled her eyes.

"Did you ever see me play?"

She studied her fingernails. "I may have caught a

game or two."

She hadn't missed a game in high school and dragged Meggy with her to see him play at BC several times during his college years. She even caught a few Tampa games after she'd gone to New York, telling herself she was only watching because it happened to be the only game on TV. She had been glued to her set the day he won his Super Bowl ring.

He would never know any of that, though.

Chapter Twelve

Finn slowed the truck on the country road and turned onto a dirt pathway leading into the pines. Passing beneath an iron archway announcing their welcome to the North Shore Boys Ranch, Cara glanced around at the scattered buildings.

A large glass and log structure sat at the center of a clearing. Several smaller cabins climbed the slope into the trees. To the right, a small lake sparkled in the summer sunlight. A football field off to the left teamed with activity as several men put dozens of teenage boys through their paces, despite the warm June day.

She shot him a smirk. "I should have known it was a football camp."

He pulled the truck to a stop next to the main building and cut the engine. "It's not just a football camp." He opened the door and climbed out. She followed. "Football teaches discipline and teamwork," he explained, "but it's just one of the activities the kids participate in while they're here."

A thin, scholarly looking man in khakis and a short-sleeved dress shirt met them on the front deck of the main building. A wide smile creased his lined face.

"Who have you brought me, Finn?"

A foot and a half shorter than the six-five Finn, the older man grinned slyly as he shook Finn's hand, his gaze remaining on Cara.

Finn laughed. "Cara, this old reprobate is the boss around here, Doc Windham. Doc, this is Cara O'Shea. She's the artist who donated those shelves I called you about."

"What an impressive place you have here." Cara shook Doc's offered hand. She was charmed when he brought her fingers to his lips for an old-world kiss on her knuckles.

His gray eyes twinkled merrily. "I'll give you a tour while Finn sees about getting those shelves unloaded." He dropped her hand. "We appreciate your thinking of us, Miss O'Shea. Our library has outgrown itself over the last couple of years. We'll put your gift to good use."

She opened her mouth to say the idea had been Finn's, when he spoke. "Don't let him talk your ear off. Doc gets caught up in his excitement over the camp's program when he has a new victim to listen to him."

Genuine affection colored Finn's tone. Doc proved the feeling was mutual, calling over his shoulders as he led Cara inside, "Put that oversized back of yours to good use and unload those shelves. I'll make sure Miss O'Shea's ears are entertained."

"Please, call me Cara." She followed him inside the combination seating and game room. Ping pong tables, dart boards, and game tables shared the space with several long, comfortable couches.

"Only if you'll call me Doc." His smile said he was pleased by the idea.

They toured the main building, and then he led her out the back door. He pointed out the classrooms and mess hall. Half a dozen canoes, stacked together against a small wooden building, marked the boathouse.

"How long have you known Finn?"

"I don't, really," she explained. "I grew up in Palmerton, so I knew *of* him. I never technically met him until about a week ago. What about you?"

"He was a student in a psychology course I taught at BC in his first year. We kept in touch over the years and became friends. I'm still a professor. I just take summers off to run the camp's program."

"How long has the camp been here?" She glanced around the orderly facility. "I grew up in Palmerton, yet never knew this place existed."

"It used to be a private camp." They strolled up a path toward several outbuildings. "This is our fifth summer. We have fifty-two boys this year. They come to us in different ways. Some through the courts, others through private requests."

"How are you funded? Are you a state program?" However they were funded, the camp was well cared for. Though the cabins lining the meandering trail weren't large, neither were they tiny.

"Some of our funding is public. The boys we get are the ones on the edge, non-dangerous kids who haven't quite gone over to the dark side, but are headed that way. When the juvenile courts think a boy can benefit from our program instead of spending time in juvenile hall, they fund his tuition here. The others are funded through private donations and fundraisers.

"The boys' dorms are here." He pointed to the closet of the cabins sitting amongst the tall pines. "The program runs for eight weeks each summer. We keep the boys on a strict schedule. Sports in the mornings, classes after lunch, and swimming or fishing before dinner. We have games and activities in the main building in the evening, but no television, video games or cell phones. We keep them pretty busy."

When they started back down the path to the main building once more, Cara commented, "I noticed the football game in progress when we pulled up. How much do you want to bet we find Finn on the sideline when we return?"

"If I know Finn, he'll be out on the field, not on the sideline." Doc smiled warmly. "His sports program is the most popular part of the camp curriculum with the boys and the key to our success. Football is the carrot we use to get them to cooperate in the academic instruction they're required to take."

"*His* sports program?" Her gaze swung to the field below. As predicted, Finn's large frame was visible at the center of the field, a group of uniform clad boys surrounding him as he demonstrated a rolling move.

Doc followed her gaze. "The camp and its program were Finn's concept. In addition, he's the major financier. He runs a weeklong football camp at the beginning of each summer. He managed to talk several of his friends from the NFL into helping out. Having that kind of one-on-one time with a famous pro hooks the boys, and once they're hooked, they're willing to put up with the academic instruction and real life counseling we require of them, in order to stay on the field."

Finn slapped one of the coaches on the back and turned to lope across the field. He smiled and waved at her and Doc, his long legs carrying him toward them.

The butterflies in her belly swarmed, leaving her a bit nauseous. God, he was gorgeous, and the more time she spent with him, the more she was beginning to believe him to be as gorgeous on the inside.

But no one was perfect. His playboy lifestyle aside, there had to be at least one major flaw somewhere. Oh, please let there be a major flaw and let her discover it soon.

Her confusion must have shown on her face. Doc cocked his head. "You didn't know this was Finn's camp?"

"He didn't mention it." Her eyes continued to follow Finn's progress across the field.

"Well, that's Finn." Doc smiled. "He doesn't advertise his connection to the camp. We could bring in a lot more money and expand if he did, but in his words, he doesn't want it to turn into a circus. The personalized atmosphere here is essential to the success of the program. For many of these kids, it's the first time in their lives anyone has given them individual attention. He's not willing to risk that by attaching his name."

A stray pass bounced to the ground several feet behind Finn. He stopped and spun around to pick up the ball. Clutching it in both hands, his big body loosened into the famous Finn form. The muscles of his back and arm bunched and stretched, and the ball sailed from his fingers in a perfect spiral. A thrilled teenager caught the pass thirty yards away.

He continued to jog up the gentle rise to the truck. When he stopped a foot away, his blue laser gaze swept her from feet to face. He lifted a hand to gently tug one of her earlobes.

"You still have your ears. Doc, you must be off your feed."

Doc snorted in false affront. She came to his defense. "Oh, I wouldn't say that. He shared some of your deep, dark secrets. Thanks for the tour, Doc…and the dirt."

Pleased, Doc winked at her. "The lunch bell is about to ring. You're welcome to stay."

Finn shook his head. "We have another appointment, but thanks."

Doc snapped his fingers. "I have a receipt for your shelves on my desk. I'll be right back." He pivoted for the main building, moving quickly for a man who had to be pushing seventy.

"What dirt?" Finn demanded the moment the screen door banged shut.

She wanted to snicker with laughter at the focused concentration on his handsome face. Instead, she gave him a silent, serene smile.

"What dirt?" He crowded closer until he loomed over her.

"Quit pestering the woman, Finn." The screen door clacked shut behind Doc. He descended the steps and handed Cara the receipt. "Thanks again for thinking of us. You come back and visit anytime."

She bent to kiss his cheek. "Thank you, Doc. I just might do that."

"You made a fan for life." Finn announced a few minutes later as he guided the truck down the dirt path to the road.

"I like him." She smiled, realizing it was true. "He has a heart for the kids here and it shows."

He nodded. "He's tough, but he has a way with the boys." He turned the truck onto the country road. "He's made a difference in a lot of troubled kids' lives."

94

He's not the only one. But she kept the thought to herself. If Finn wanted to keep his altruistic acts quiet, she would respect his wishes.

"What dirt?" he asked again, and she didn't fight the laugh this time.

"Paranoid, Finnegan?"

"Persistent."

That persistence made her wonder just what kind of dirt he was worried about. "Why don't you tell me what you *think* he told me, and I'll tell you if you're right."

"Oh ho." His low chuckled danced over her nerve endings. "Beautiful and sneaky. A deadly combination. I like it." She snorted. He cajoled. "Come on, O'Shea."

"Give it up, Finnegan." She smiled. "I know how to keep a secret."

His narrowed eyes sparkled with challenging humor. "I'll have to dig up some dirt on you, and then we'll see how well you keep secrets."

"Good luck with that." She smirked and crossed her arms, confident *that* wouldn't happen.

"I'm Erin's favorite new cousin. She'll give up the goods." He grinned at her sudden frown.

She wouldn't put it past her sister to give Finn any dirt she recalled, just for the entertainment value. Not that there was any dirt to be told, other than mooning over him most of her life, which Erin didn't know about, thank God. Cara couldn't think of anything embarrassing enough to be concerned over. He already knew about the most embarrassing moment of her life. He witnessed it, and she had learned enough about him to come to the conclusion he wasn't cruel. He hadn't mentioned that night and wouldn't.

Confidence made her smile smug. "I'm an open book, Finnegan. Dig all you want."

****

Finn waited until she disappeared inside her studio before pulling onto the road. She had been truly relaxed for the first time since he met her, talking, laughing, and trading quips. With her usual hostility on hold, he'd gotten a glimpse of the woman behind the prickly mask she wore. He was determined to see more.

Damn, he wanted to kiss her again. Only the memory of the edgy panic in her wide eyes after the last time, kept him from acting on the desire, but it wasn't in his nature to wait very long for something he wanted. He wanted Cara O'Shea.

It pleased him inordinately to learn she had watched him on the field occasionally. And wasn't that sad? He would take any attention he could get from her, even if it was from years earlier. Damn, he was pitiful. He consoled himself with the knowledge that he had her attention now, and he meant to have a lot more of it before he was through.

Chapter Thirteen

Dappled sunlight skittered and danced through the trees as Cara slipped on a pair of oversized sunglasses and crossed the grassy lawn of Cookson Park. Fifty yards away, Tom paced beneath a grand maple, its mighty arms spread wide to embrace the warm summer afternoon. She swallowed against surging nerves as he swiped at his brow with a handkerchief before tucking it back in the pocket of his light-weight dress slacks.

Though she wasn't late, he twisted his wrist to check his watch. Was he nervous, or did he think she wouldn't show? The latter probably, considering he'd all but bullied her into this meeting and agreeing to meet with him was more than she had given him in years.

She studied him as she drew near. Other than his graying hair, which had once been the same dark red as her own, he'd changed little in her absence. He still sported the strong physique she remembered, with wide shoulders and the muscled arms she'd run to as a child. From the time she could remember, she'd trusted him to always make things right in her world.

She'd been shattered when he betrayed that trust.

Unlike Shan and Erin, who resembled the petite Mary in looks and build, Cara was pure Tom, including his unusual height. At six foot six, he had first-hand knowledge of what she went through as a child, always being the tallest kid in class. They shared a special bond. Even when no one else understood, he always did.

When she was struggling through her teenage years, and her curvy body developed and began to draw the interest of males on a regular basis, he'd stepped in numerous times to glare down young, or not so young, would-be bucks. She eventually found her own way to handle the unwanted attention, mostly by pretending to ignore the blatant stares and the suggestive comments. In addition, she did her best to avoid drawing attention by dressing in curve concealing clothes, and hiding out with her paintbrushes and easels.

But through it all, Tom had been so much more to her than a loving father. He'd been her own personal superhero.

He ripped the rug out from under her when he turned out to be less than perfect.

For the past eight years, she avoided all but the most obligatory contact with him, and he had let her, but she was back now and living in the same small town. It was inevitable their lives would intertwine, whether she wished so or not. Logic said it was necessary they come to some kind of workable solution to their estrangement, but the heart didn't always adhere to logic.

Relief and nerves flooded his familiar face when he spotted her walking toward him. She stopped several feet away.

His smile was strained but hopeful. "Thank you for coming."

"I said I would."

"Thank you, anyway." He gestured to the bench behind him. She shook her head. "I'm sorry, Cara mine." She didn't pull away from his touch when he brushed his knuckles against her cheek, but she didn't speak either. He sighed. "I hurt you. I hurt Mary and your sisters, and I live with that knowledge every day. I can't change what happened, but if I can convince you of anything, I would hope it would be that I love all of you, and knowing I've caused you hurt is a cross I'll bear until the day I die."

"You love all of us," she murmured. "You love Ma, so you snuck around and slept with another woman. Yeah, Daddy. I can see how much you love us."

Ruddy color crept into his cheeks and his voice went sharp. "Hold it, little girl. I know you're hurt and angry, and you're entitled to feel that way, but the situation is complicated enough without you questioning my love for you. I do love you, more than my own life. Don't ever doubt that."

Matching his angry stare, she lifted her chin. "Then tell me why, Daddy, because I don't understand how you could have done what you did, if you love us the way you say you do."

His shoulders stiffened, but he didn't argue her point. "Will you sit?"

"I'd rather stand."

"Do you mind if I do?" She shook her head. He sank to the bench and sucked air through his teeth. "I met Hannah my senior year of high school."

Cara crossed her arms. "Ma mentioned something like that.

His eyes widened briefly in surprise. "I met her on

Labor Day, the day before school began my senior year. She had just moved to town and came up to the soda counter at the diner where I was working. She ordered a coke. I fell in love with her the moment I saw her."

Pain pierced Cara's heart, making breathing difficult. She lifted her head to the breeze and turned her back on him. Moving over to the tree several feet away, she wrapped one arm around the broad trunk and leaned against it.

"I'm not trying to hurt you, Cara. I'm trying to explain," he said softly. She didn't reply. After a moment's hesitation, he continued. "Hannah's father had just been killed in a boating accident, and she and her mother moved back to town to live with Hanna's grandparents. The Dunns were the richest family in town. She came into the diner with her mother. The woman stunk of old money. Her mother didn't even see me as I filled their orders. I was a seventeen-year-old kid, working at a soda counter. So far beneath her notice, it was as if I weren't there. Hannah noticed me, though. She smiled and thanked me when I handed her their drinks. You can't imagine how surprised and thrilled I was the next morning when I walked into class and there was Hannah, sitting in the front row. She smiled at me as I walked passed her to my desk, and I was lost."

Cara dug her nails into the trunk of the tree and squeezed her eyes shut.

"From that point on we were inseparable, much to her mother's frustration. She forbade Hannah from seeing me, but we were in love. Hannah defied her mother, sneaking out to be with me every chance she got. My eighteenth birthday came, and we made plans to sneak off and get married the day she turned eighteen as well."

Married? Cara's eyes popped open and she swung her head around to stare at him. He gazed off into the distance as though reliving the past.

"Then, three weeks before her birthday, Hannah disappeared. I was frantic. I went to the big house where she lived with her mother and grandparents. Her mother was expecting me. She met me at the door, informing me that Hannah had gone to live with her grandparents on their estate somewhere in the Caribbean."

He sat forward, propping his elbows on his knees, his hands dangling between them. He dropped his gaze to stare at the ground. The despondency of the motion sliced at her heart. She pushed away from the tree and crossed the grassy path to sit beside him on the bench. He turned his head to look at her and there was hell in his eyes.

"I was eighteen, Cara mine. I had no money and no way of tracking her down." He slumped back against the bench and stared up through the branches of the tree. "I knew in my heart she would never have left without a word. Not unless she was forced. But after six months, I had no choice but to accept I was never going to see her again. I still had my scholarship, and when fall came, I packed up my belongings and went to college. You've heard the story of how your mother and I met. I was given a second chance at love when I met your mother, but I never could forget Hannah."

Straightening, he laid his hand on hers where she held them clenched on her lap. "You've never been in love, so you can't understand the strength of that first time. Your mother and I made a life together, and when you girls came along, I knew I'd been given a gift beyond measure. I loved Mary. I still do. How could I not? But the love I have for her isn't the same as the soul stealing need buried deep in my heart for the girl I had thought to spend my life with, only to have her stolen from me before we ever had a chance to begin that life."

He patted her hand before moving his own away. Shoving his fingers through his hair in agitation, he leaned his elbows on his knees once more and stared toward a young family in the distance. "Fate stepped in when I bought the accounting agency here in Palmerton. I placed an ad in the town paper for a secretary. Hannah answered the ad. It was hard to tell which of us was more shocked. She hadn't known I was the new owner and stopped in the office to fill out an application. She walked in the open doorway, stood in the middle of the office, and started to cry. That day was one of the best, and worst, of my life."

Cara sucked in a ragged breath. "Why hadn't she ever gotten in touch with you?"

"She was just a girl when her family whisked her off to the Virgin Islands. She managed to get to a phone once, but before she could reach me, she was discovered by her grandmother. They watched her from then on. The next few years weren't easy for her."

Cara stifled a snort. The last *eight* years hadn't exactly been a picnic for Ma and the rest of them. "How so?"

He sighed, but held her demanding gaze. "The experiences of those years were Hannah's own personal hell, and aren't mine to share, even to win your sympathy. I've experienced her family first hand. Suffice to say, they're a viciously controlling, cruel bunch. She did what they told her. She went to school, got her degree in business, and when she graduated, they set up a job for her here in the states with her family's financial firm. They put her on a plane back to Maine. When it landed in New York, she didn't get on the connecting flight. She simply walked away. By that time, I had met and married your mother. When Hannah managed to make her way back to Maine and learned I'd married, she left the area and her family, and never returned. She eventually settled here in Palmerton."

And destroyed our family. Helpless anger shimmered through Cara. "So, what happened? You hired her as your secretary and started having an affair?"

Other than a slight flinch, he didn't react to her cutting sarcasm. "I hired her, but there was no affair. Not at first. She refused the job, but I kept after her until she finally relented. I begged her, Cara. I still loved her. I wanted her in my life any way I could have her. I convinced her, and myself, it would be enough just to see her every day. For a while it was. Then your mother went back to school, and I found myself alone more often than not."

Hot fury burst within Cara. She leapt to her feet and rounded on him. "Don't you dare! Damn it, Daddy. Don't you dare blame Ma for any of this!"

"I'm not." He rose to stand in front of her. "It's hard for a man to admit, even to himself, when push came to shove, he wasn't strong enough to do what was right for his family. But then, I knew at the time no matter what I chose to do, someone was going to be hurt. I'll go to my grave knowing I chose to save myself from the worst of that hurt and sacrificed Mary and you girls in the process." He shoved both hands through his hair. "I'm the one to blame, Cara mine. Not your mother and not Hannah." At her snort of disdain, he laid his hand on her arm to keep her from spinning away. "I know you won't believe me, but Hannah doesn't deserve your animosity. She did everything she could to prevent anyone from being hurt, and is just as much a victim as Mary and you girls. *I* was the one who forced the situation."

He was right. Cara didn't believe him. No matter what kind of face he put on it, Hannah Dunn had stolen another woman's husband and destroyed a family. Cara tugged free of his hand.

He dropped his arm to his side with a heavy sigh. "I used your mother's absence as an excuse to have what I wanted, what I'd wanted most of my life. I pressured Hannah until she finally couldn't take it anymore. She turned in her resignation. She was going to leave town."

"Why didn't you let her?" Cara cried. Eight years of heartbreak and disillusionment converged and left her shaking. She shoved at him with all her might and he staggered back. Her face twisted in a mask of pain, and furious tears blurred her vision. She leaped at him, thumping both fists against his chest. "Why didn't you just let her?"

Her voice broke on a sob. He pulled her into his arms and held her close, pressing his face into her hair. Standing there in the shade of the old maple, he rocked her back and forth as she wept. She clung to him as she had when she was a little girl and needed him to make everything all right. But he couldn't make everything right this time.

"I couldn't lose her again, Cara mine." Pain and loss strangled his voice. "I'd made a good life with your mother. You girls were my joy. But I couldn't lose her again."

Chapter Fourteen

The tightly shuttered windows made the studio dark, despite sunset being several hours away. Cara's muscles ached as if she had been run over by a truck and Daddy didn't appear much better when she left him.

She now had a better understanding of why he did the things he'd done. Still, she didn't know yet how, or even *if*, that understanding would change her feelings about the situation.

Hearing her father professing love at first sight for a woman other than Ma was like taking a fist to the heart, but he was wrong when he said she couldn't understand the strength of a first love. She did understand.

As a woman, she knew the folly of loving a man like Finn, but if seeing him again had taught her anything, it was that the long held feelings she had for him hadn't faded with time, despite her efforts to put him from her mind and heart. Her father's declaration of that same kind of love for a woman Cara thought of only in terms of infidelity, just confused her more than she had already been.

Too strung out to deal with her father's revelations, or her helpless feelings for Finn, she needed to paint. With that in mind, she tossed her purse and keys on a shelf and headed for her easel. She stumbled to a halt, yelping in terror when a large body rose from behind the counter in the center of the room.

Recognizing Finn in the dim light did nothing to calm her racing heart. "Are you crazy? You scared the hell out of me!"

"I can see that." Calmness itself, he leaned on the counter with a crowbar in one hand.

"What are you doing here?"

He lifted the crowbar. "Just cleaning up the rest of the carpet tacking."

"In the dark?"

Hadn't Ryan finished that task this morning before he left? She eyed Finn suspiciously. With her heartbeat just barely returning to normal, she stomped over to the wall and slapped the light switch, flooding the room with light.

"How did you get in here?" She jammed her fists to her hips. "Breaking and entering is a crime."

"You don't say?"

"Are you stalking me?"

"Looks like it." He shrugged.

"There are laws against that kind of thing, you know."

"Are you going to call the cops? My cousin is the chief. I could get him for you on his private cell phone."

Relief and the drop of adrenaline from the fright he had given her must be making her lightheaded. She shook her head and tried not to smile. She failed.

"Small towns," she grumbled beneath her breath.

"What was that?" Though his smile was teasing, his eyes were intent and she knew he noticed her red rimmed eyes. He didn't comment on her tear ravaged face, and she was thankful for his restraint.

"I asked how you got in here. I know I locked the doors before I left."

Shoving his fingers into the front pocket of his jeans, he held up a ring holding two keys and jangled them slightly.

"I used my key."

"Your key? I didn't give you a key!" Indignation smothered any lingering lightheadedness.

He rolled one shoulder in an abbreviated shrug. "I had them from when I did the renovation on the bookstore. I guess I never returned them."

She held out her hand, palm up in silent demand. He slipped the ring back into his front pocket.

She glared at him. "Add new door locks to your bid."

He pulled a small, tattered notebook from his back pocket. Taking a pen from the counter top, he flipped to the top page.

"New locks." He scribbled in the book. "Extra set of keys for the contractor."

A knock on the front door prevented her from commenting. She crossed the room, thankful for the interruption. The jerk. He needed a set of keys during the renovation, and they both knew it. Whoever was knocking had saved her from having to return them to him later.

Cara opened the door and Meggy sailed inside. She took one look at Cara's face and grabbed her close.

"Aw, honey. Are you okay?"

"I'm fine." Cara tossed a worried glance over her shoulder, embarrassed to have Finn witness to the third degree she knew would be coming. Meggy had called just before Cara left to meet Tom, and she wasn't surprised her friend showed up here instead of calling to find out what happened.

"You don't *look* fine." Meggy held up a large bottle of cheap chardonnay with a grin. "But, never fear. I've brought medicine." Her grin froze as she spotted Finn. Gleeful speculation sparkled in her eyes when they jerked back to Cara. "Hmmm. Looks like the doctor is already here. Hi, Finn. I didn't see you there."

Cara flashed Meggy a horrified glare and turned. The amusement shining in Finn's blue eyes said he heard every word.

"Hi, Meggy. How've you been?"

"I've been great, thanks." She shot Cara a what's-going-on stare before cocking her head and smiling at Finn. "What are you doing here?"

"Meggy..."

Finn spoke over Cara's growled warning. "I'm doing the renovations on Cara's studio."

Meggy whipped her head around. "*Finn the Fine* is your contractor?"

Cara groaned, her eyes sliding shut. She wasn't going to look at him. She really wasn't. She opened her eyes. The satisfied smile on his face should have warned her of what was coming.

"Remember that dirt?" he quipped softly.

She wanted to laugh, despite the heat rising up her chest and face. Instead, she turned to Meggy, who was already backing toward the front door.

"Oh, no you don't." Cara scrambled after her, planning to keep her from leaving by sitting on her if necessary.

"Will you look at that?" Meggy glanced at her watch much too quickly to have noted the time. "I forgot I'm supposed to be meeting with, um..." She snapped her fingers. "With Shan! To talk about that idea we discussed the other day." She thrust the bottle of wine into Cara's hand and rushed out the door, calling over her shoulder. "I'll talk to you tomorrow."

Cara squeezed her eyes shut for a moment when the door closed in her face. Clutching the bottle to her chest, she faced Finn. He stood with his arms crossed, his weight cocked on one hip, and a dimpled grin on his face.

She stalked passed him to grab her purse and keys, meaning to make a clean getaway to her upstairs apartment.

"Finn the Fine?"

"Nobody takes Meggy seriously." She continued toward the stairs, too heartsick and drained from the conversation with her father to enjoy the bantering tone in Finn's voice. If she couldn't paint, then she wanted to crawl into bed and pull the covers over her head.

"So, you think of me as Finn the Fine?" His voice was gently teasing and close, telling her he followed her to the stairs. She stopped and turned. Sure enough, he was only a foot away. She met his gaze, but didn't return his smile.

"I don't think of you that way anymore." This wasn't a subject she wanted to get into with him—ever, but especially not now, when she was so raw and ragged inside.

"Not so fine anymore, huh?" He pushed the subject.

"Something like that." *Please, just let it go.* But of

course, he didn't.

"When did you stop thinking of me as Finn the Fine?"

She stiffened and knew she paled. She'd been foolish to think he wasn't cruel enough to bring up that night, and in his defense, he didn't realize what he was asking, but that didn't help at the moment. Still, she should have known the topic would come up eventually. That night would always stand between them.

She swallowed the remembered humiliation rising like a fountain within her. Her voice was low and rough when she answered. "Graduation night, eight years ago."

"Yeah," he said quietly. "We've never talked about that night, have we?" Comprehension darkened his blue eyes, even as his smile faded.

"And we aren't going to." She turned to leave. He stopped her by wrapping his long fingers around her upper arm. She glanced down at his hand and sighed. "I'm tired, Finn. Lock the door on your way out."

He didn't release her. Instead, the tip of his finger moved her chin to face him. "Hey." He cupped her cheek, his thumb rubbing across her cheekbone in a gentle caress. He released her arm to frame her face with his palms. "Do you know what I remember from that night?"

She lifted her chin in heated defiance. "A drunk, half naked, genetic freak?"

"Genetic freak? What the hell?" His narrowed eyes were so focused on her she wanted to shrink from the intensity of them. When he spoke, his words were crisp and clear. "I remember a frightened, seventeen-year-old girl with the body of a goddess and the regality of a queen, facing down a pack of idiot teenage boys. You were thrust into a situation that would have made anyone cower, Cara, and yet you stood there with your quiet dignity, and shamed everyone."

She searched his face with wary eyes, seeking the truth that would put a lie to his words—words that oozed over her memory of that night like a healing balm. She found only sincerity.

He explored her face with his eyes, from her brows, over her cheekbones to her mouth. When his eyes rose again to meet hers, her breath caught at the burning desire in them. Her heart galloped like a wild horse in her chest.

"You took my breath away that night, Cara." Slowly, he lowered his head until his mouth was a whisper from hers. "You still take my breath away."

His mouth covered hers. He didn't touch her anywhere but where his hands rested against her face and where his lips rubbed across hers. As with the last kiss, fire exploded through her system, urging her to press closer until nothing separated them and she could once again feel the hard angles of his body molding to her soft curves. She whimpered softly at the loss when his mouth left hers, only then realizing her eyes had drifted shut at the first brush of his mouth. They fluttered open to find him watching her.

The hot blue flame of desire burning in his eyes seduced her, and her heart soared. She was completely off balance, suffering residual emotion from talking to her father, but that didn't matter. Even if it was only for this moment, she didn't want to resist Finn's seduction. She'd loved him for so long—wanted to hold him, to be held by him, and know the joy of becoming one with him.

Acting on those wants might be the mistake of her life, but she was beyond caring. She rose on her tiptoes and pressed her mouth to his.

His lips crushed hers, while his arms wrapped around her and pulled her so tightly to him, the powerful thud of his heart thundered against her breasts. He urged her mouth open, and shyly her tongue met the demanding thrust of his. When he broke the kiss to lean his forehead on hers, she swayed in his arms, dazed and confused.

"Let me love you, Cara."

She thrilled at the husky timber of his voice. Nuzzling her forehead to his, she spoke from the heart, knowing he wouldn't understand the deeper meaning of her words. "I want you to love me."

He compressed her ribs in a bone crushing squeeze before loosening his hold enough for her to breathe. He dropped his chin to the top of her head. "Are you sure?"

She nodded.

"Then we'd better find a bed, or we're going to end up on your hardwood floor."

Chapter Fifteen

Untangling from his arms, she stepped back, the forgotten bottle of wine dangling from her fingers. He sighed inwardly. Had she changed her mind? Did she mean to call a halt to the madness gripping them both? Relief crashed through him when she wrapped her fingers around his, and led him up the stairs to her apartment.

Neither of them spoke until she stopped beside a queen-sized bed in her small bedroom. She set the wine bottle on the nightstand and gazed at him. Her beautiful eyes suddenly filled with uncertainty.

"I don't know what to do."

He stilled and narrowed his attention on her face. Her nervousness broadcast itself in the lowering of her eyes, the blush on her cheeks. Every raging instinct in his body ground to a halt.

Jesus, was she a virgin?

He couldn't wrap his mind around the concept. She stood beside her bed, this woman with a body designed to temp men to sin, and stared at him with the eyes of an innocent. He should end this now, while he still could.

Hell, who was he kidding? He had passed the stopping stage when she led him up those stairs.

Inhaling a deep breath and forcing his overheated

body to relax, he ran a soothing hand over her shoulder, down her arm and up again.

"Have you ever been with a man, baby?"

"I...yes, once." Two flags of color bloomed on her cheeks. Her eyes slid shut.

His heart was going to explode in his chest.

"Hey." She continued to stand before him with her eyes squeezed tight. "Hey." She opened her eyes. He cocked his head and tried to reassure her. "It's like riding a bike. Once you've learned..."

She laughed as he meant her to. "I'm nervous."

Lifting her hand, he pressed her palm against his chest, directly above his frantically beating heart. Her eyes widened in surprise.

"Me too. We'll take it slow. If I do something you don't like, tell me. If I do something you like, feel free to beg for more." He grinned unapologetically, pleased when the nerves faded from her eyes with a smile.

Leaving her hand over his heart, he reached for the top button of her blouse. She stood silently while his fingers dispensed with each of the tiny buttons. In no time, he peeled back the lapels and surveyed what he exposed.

"You're beautiful."

He bent at the knees, leaning forward to glide his lips along her delicate collarbone. The open material of her blouse slid over the velvet soft skin of her shoulders at the urging of his hands, riding his wrists until it slithered down her arms to drop to the floor on a whisper.

Her head dropped back helplessly when his mouth moved to one shoulder, nipping gently at the sensitive tendon there. She shivered.

"I've wanted to do this almost from the first time I saw you." With his tongue, he laved at the nip, leaving a warm, moist trail as he explored her neck.

She swayed against him, and he lifted his head. He studied the color across her cheekbones before his gaze dropped to her breasts, half hidden from his hungry view by a frilly confection of white silk and lace. His gaze continued down over her flat stomach to the clasp at the top of the white Capri pants molding her curves like a jealous lover.

The button and zipper fell victim to his experienced fingers, and sliding his palms over her hips, he peeled away the light material until her slacks joined the blouse on the floor. A low groan escaped him and every muscle in his body tightened with his first look at Cara O'Shea in nothing but a white lace demi-bra and thong.

He wanted to swallow her whole.

****

His eyes, when they met hers, were a piercing, laser blue. She went into his arms amazed and pleased she had put that fire in them. His kiss was urgent, and spoke of a hunger she understood. Just as hungry for the taste and feel of him, her fingers jerked at the material of his shirt as he lowered her gently to the bed.

He levered his body away from hers, and with one muscular arm, yanked the shirt up and over his head. Rippling muscle and sinew, perfectly formed and forged by years of intense athletic training, made her sigh in helpless appreciation. Fascinated, she caressed the light spray of dark curls, brushing testing strokes over the solid muscle.

His crooked, dimpled smile encouraged her to

continue her exploration, and her fingers followed the narrow band of hair down from his chest to where the trail disappeared behind the snap of his jeans. Taut stomach muscles quivered at her light touch, and when her fingers hesitated at his navel, he met her gaze.

His voice was graveled and his eyes dark. "It's up to you, baby. We're going wherever you want to go."

"I wouldn't complain if you kissed me again."

He grinned, and complied. As he made love to her mouth, her hands roamed, brushing, squeezing, flexing against the strength so evident in his back and chest. Before long, the pleasant exploration wasn't enough, and she broke her mouth away to stare up at him, her breathing erratic.

She attacked the snap of his jeans shamelessly, and smiled at his encouraging, dark laugh. His hands joined hers in her haste, shoving his jeans down over his hips. With a quick twist and a well-placed kick, the denim went flying off the foot of the bed and a nearly naked Finn leaned over her. He slipped a thickly muscled thigh between her legs.

It was an unfamiliar sensation, to feel small and vulnerable, and she found to her amazement, the awareness only increased her excitement. The width of his shoulders all but eclipsed the dimming afternoon light from the window behind him, and she shuddered when the tips of his fingers traced the skin just above the lace of her bra.

With his eyes burning into hers, he hooked a finger in the lacy material, tugging until a rosy nipple popped free. He dipped his dark head, and her breath caught at the stab of his tongue on the tightened bud. Her sigh came out in a ragged whoosh when he blew a gentle breath across the rosy crest. He flashed her a dizzying smile before lowering his head once more and taking her full into his mouth.

Heat exploded through her like a flash fire. She arched her back, and thrilled at his deep rumble of encouragement. He flicked open the front clasp of her bra to brush away the frilly barrier and treated her other breast to the same adoration.

Fingers buried in his thick hair, she held his head to her as he feasted on her heated flesh. She moaned in disappointment when his mouth retreated, and he laughed wickedly. Trailing a nibble of kisses down the fluttering muscles of her stomach, he paused at her navel, devoting time to that mysterious dimple. His mouth left a heated trail downward, pausing at the band of her panties. He fingered the tiny scrap of lace and met her gaze from beneath sensually lowered lashes.

"Do we need these?"

Unable to speak, she shook her head, and he peeled the thong down her legs. Without breaking eye contact, he leaned forward to press a kiss to the auburn curls hiding her most secret place.

When she closed her eyes and shuddered, the bed moved as he levered up and left her. Her eyes flew open to find him standing at the foot of the bed. He met her gaze, bending to pick up his jeans and pull several packets from the pocket. Walking to the side of the bed, he dropped them on the nightstand, before tossing the jeans to the floor once more. She swallowed as he pushed his navy briefs down over his hips and kicked out of them, then stood there letting her look her fill.

She stared, eyes wide.

He'd always been beautiful to her, but naked, he

was beyond words. His body was surely the way God had intended the male form to be. Like a warrior of old, he carried the scars of battle, including the angry slash bisecting his left knee. The imperfections only added to the impression of pure male strength.

Below impossibly wide shoulders, his strong arms resembled sculpted teakwood. Dark hair sprinkled the muscled plates of his chest, spreading to each tight nipple and running down in a thin line to flare once at his navel and again at his groin. His chest tapered to ridged stomach muscles and lean hips. Between long, thick thighs, the proof of his desire stood strong and intimidating.

Though she didn't ask, she wished he would turn around. She'd had a thing for his butt since the first time she saw him in those shiny white football pants. But a butt view would be overkill at this point, when she was already struggling to breathe.

Without a word, he placed a knee on the side of the bed. Leaning down, he feasted his way up her body. His mouth tasted the skin at her shins and knees, thighs and hips. He lingered over her stomach and breasts, her shoulders and neck. Everywhere he ventured, he called forth another shockingly exciting response. His mouth tasted, his hands molded and tested, he even used his body to stoke the flames threatening to burn her alive. Like a master musician he played her, with the nuzzle of a scratchy jaw here, and the rub of muscled thigh there, and by the time his mouth claimed hers once again, she writhed beneath him.

Her hands raced over his broad shoulders and grasped at his thick biceps, trying to drag him closer. Frantically, her body arched into his until he settled himself between her thighs and closed his mouth over hers in a kiss that brought her molten bones to flash point.

She whimpered, and her fingernails left tiny crescents where they dug into the muscled strength of his arms. Lifting his head, he rose above her. His eyes never leaving hers, he grabbed a packet from the nightstand. Strong white teeth ripped at the foil, and levering on one muscled arm, he covered himself.

Though dazed with passion, she knew some of her sudden nervousness must have shown in her eyes, when he paused to softly kiss her mouth in reassurance.

"I won't hurt you, Cara. I promise."

The ripple of desire coursing through his big body when he resettled himself against her feminine cradle did more to calm her nerves than his words. *She'd* done that to him. A sense of feminine power filled her, and she reveled in the knowledge she wasn't the only one drowning in this river of need.

Bracing on his forearms, he linked his fingers with hers. She smiled at him. He lowered his head to cover her mouth, merging her throaty moan with his as he slipped inside her.

The blind pleasure of being one with the man she'd loved most of her life nearly left her breathless, and when he began to move, she did indeed know what to do. She met and matched him in the sensual dance, and when she reached paradise, hurtling over the edge, she took him with her.

****

Finn brushed a hand along the bed beside him and found the space empty. Rolling to his back, he opened his eyes to the faint lightening of dawn. He wasn't surprised to discover Cara gone. Despite several mind blowing bouts of lovemaking throughout the night, she hadn't been able to rest when he finally left her alone. She disappeared sometime after he collapsed into sleep.

Her conversation with Tom continued to weigh on her mind. She looked like hell warmed over when she walked through the door late yesterday afternoon, and though he hadn't meant to take advantage of her vulnerability, he didn't regret he had. He was male enough, arrogant enough, to use whatever means were at his disposal to get what he wanted. He couldn't remember ever wanting anyone as badly as Cara O'Shea.

Flipping back the sheet, he pulled on his rumpled jeans and went in search of coffee and Cara. Ten minutes later, two mugs of coffee in hand, he found her in the unfinished studio.

Pausing at the bottom of the steps, his gaze was drawn across the darkened expanse of the room to the small island of light cast by a single, ancient floor lamp. She stood with her back to him, her curvy, yet slender form bathed in the soft glow as she studied the canvas in front of her.

His admiring gaze ran down the fall of dark red curls flowing unfettered down her back. The hem of a man's chambray shirt stopped at mid-thigh, leaving her long, well-toned legs bare beneath the light blue material. Who had donated the shirt? Had it belonged to the one man she'd been with in the past?

Her artless confession of having been with a man only once before answered the question of her seeming innocence, but didn't explain it. Cara wasn't the type of woman men would ignore. From her unreceptive behavior toward him, up until last night, it was safe to assume she'd been the one doing the ignoring. How, and more importantly, why would a woman as passionate as Cara proved to be, avoid the normal male-female relationships one would expect of a woman of her age and looks?

She leaned forward in the weak light to narrow her eyes at the canvas, exposing several more inches of gut wrenching leg. He squashed the kernel of jealousy forming in his gut for the shirt's owner. After all, Finn was the one enjoying the view now.

"I'd suggest opening a shutter to let in some light, but I wouldn't want to have to fight off every male in town when they get a look at you in that outfit."

She spun around, startled, and her smile was shy as he walked to her.

Padding to her on silent, bare feet, he pressed a kiss to her forehead, then handed her a mug. "I thought I'd find you here."

He turned to study the canvas. Though the painting wasn't completed, she accomplished a lot in the time since she left him sleeping in her bed. There was a compelling sadness in the scene she'd created, that was reflected in her solemn face.

"I didn't want to disturb you. I was..." She shrugged, a nervous gesture. "Restless."

Finn nodded toward the easel. "So, this is an example of a genuine O'Shea, is it?"

She dropped her paintbrush in a jar of cleaning solution. "I paint what I feel."

She had depicted Tom, leaning forward on a park bench beneath a big maple, his elbows resting on his knees, while his head hung in dejection.

"And what were you feeling here?" He motioned to the canvas with the mug in his hand. "Hopeless?"

She shot him a sideways glance. Her eyes were haunted. They skittered back to the canvas. She didn't reply.

"It's rough on a man's ego when a woman slips from his arms and suffers from hopelessness."

Her gaze jerked back to him. "Oh, Finn. No." She shook her head, resting a hand on his bare chest. "No, last night was wonderful."

"I was kidding, Cara." He smiled. "You're so intense. I was trying to lighten the mood." He brushed his knuckles across her cheek. "As for last night, we were pretty damned incredible together, and I don't need you to admit it to know you thought so too." He glanced around the empty room, and then slid a hip onto the counter to sit. "Who's your decorator? You need some chairs around here."

She set her mug on the counter beside him, and picked up a rag to wipe her paint stained fingers. "I plan to get some as soon as my contractor gets his butt moving and finishes my studio."

He squinted over his coffee mug in mock insult, and she smiled. "Will you show it to Tom when it's done?"

She tossed the rag on the counter, and wrapped her fingers around her mug. "I have no idea what I'm going to do. With the painting or anything else. You're pretty perceptive for a jock. Hopeless was exactly what I was feeling when I picked up the brush this morning. The conversation with my father kept running through my head like a haunting." She sighed. "I'm more confused now than I was before talking to him."

"I can imagine. I would think infidelity would leave a person with a wide range of strong emotions. Look how pissed off I was when you accused me of doing the same thing."

Her chin rose. "I apologized for that."

"Yes, you did." He winked. "And very sweetly, I might add."

She snorted. "I was not sweet. I was really mad at you, and you weren't very nice when I was trying to apologize."

He smiled at her grumbling tone. "No, I wasn't. That's my point. I was furious over just the idea. You've had to deal with the reality of it for years."

She stared at the painting. "I haven't been dealing with it," she murmured. "I haven't for years. I should have faced my father a long time ago, instead of running off to New York and burying myself in school and my art, but I couldn't."

"You're dealing with it now."

Her laugh was harsh. "Like I said, I'm more confused than ever."

He sat his mug aside and hopped off the counter, enfolding her in his arms. "Don't be so hard on yourself, O'Shea. You'll figure it out."

She tilted her head back to gaze into his face. "Have you always been such an optimist?"

He smiled devilishly as he bumped his hips against hers. "After last night, do you even have to ask?"

Laughing, she reached around him, her mug clattering on the surface of the counter. She filtered her fingers through his hair and pulled his head down, pressing her mouth to his. Unlike the night before, they didn't make it to her bed.

Chapter Sixteen

"Okay, spill it."

Flipping down the lid, Meggy settled herself on Cara's closed toilet and crossed her arms. Cara shot Shan a pleading stare where she leaned against the open bathroom door. Her sister rolled her shoulders in a helpless shrug.

Cara rolled her eyes, supremely glad Finn needed to catch an early morning flight to shoot a commercial in Los Angeles.

"For crying out loud." Wrapped in a towel, wet hair dripping in her eyes, she dragged a second towel from the rack on the wall and climbed from the shower. She shouldered her way passed Shan into her bedroom. "Do you two mind if I get dressed before you grill me?"

"You know we aren't going anywhere until you tell us." Meggy swept into the room with Shan on her heels. "You might as well start talking."

Cara bent at the waist to wrap up her hair in the towel. She straightened in time to see Shan's eyes widen when they landed on the disheveled bed. She gawked wordlessly at the two pillows, both showing signs of having had a head resting there recently.

Meggy didn't suffer from a loss of words. She shrieked. "Oh! My! God! You had sex with Finn the Fine?"

Cara groaned, snatching her frilly yellow robe from a hook on the door. Dropping her towel, she shoved her arms in the sleeves and yanked the belt closed. The slow heat staining her cheeks ruined the mulish glare she turned on her friend, and did nothing to shut her up.

"Well, it's about damn time."

"What do you mean, it's about time?" Shan's brow wrinkled in confusion. "She just met him last week at the rehearsal dinner." She turned puzzled green eyes on Cara. "You just met him at the rehearsal dinner, right?"

Meggy didn't give Cara a chance to respond. "Oh, please. Are you blind? Your sister has had the hots for Palmerton's resident stud for a little longer than two weeks." She slapped her hands to her hips and rolled her eyes at Cara's fulminating glare. "That cat's totally out of the bag already, since you had *sex* with him. Holy shit, I still can't believe you had *sex* with him!"

"Will you stop saying that!" Cara stormed passed them, hurrying out the door for the kitchen.

"What cat?" Shan followed. "What's going on?"

"Nothing." Cara tucked an errant strand of hair into the towel.

"Your sister has been in love with Michael Finnegan since the sixth grade," Meggy announced gleefully, entering the kitchen to pull the orange juice from the fridge. She opened the top and swigged straight from the carton.

"What are you, a guy? Give me that!" Cara yanked the carton from Meggy's hand. "That's disgusting."

Meggy smirked and shrugged.

"Sixth grade?" Shan demanded.

"Your sister got an eyeful of Finn and Alice Butler in a heavy duty clutch behind the gymnasium after a game one night." Meggy grinned at Shan. "She took one look at him in his football uniform and fell in looove." She ignored Cara's glare. "Sooo, how was he?"

Cara shut her eyes.

"Sixth grade?" Shan repeated, her voice rising.

"God, he's gorgeous." Meggy wiggled her brows. "I'll bet he's even better naked. He is, isn't he?"

Cara slapped the carton of juice down and leaned both palms against the edge of the counter. She dropped her head back on her shoulders "Okay! Okay! I've had a thing for him since the sixth grade, and he was amazing and..." She blew out a breath and glanced over her shoulder. "I can't even *begin* to tell you how good he looks naked."

"I knew it!" Meggy punched a fist in the air.

Cara coughed a short laugh, turned, and then slumped against the counter. "I am so screwed."

"What?" Shan shook her head. "Why are you screwed?"

"What do you mean?" Meggy twisted her lips comically.

Cara met Meggy's gaze, and years of memories were there between them. This morning Cara awakened beside Finn's big, beautiful body and knew the feelings she carried in her heart for the man all these years had only been a trial run for the real thing.

"I'm in love with him," she said starkly.

"Of course you are." Meggy snorted. "You've been in love with him for years."

"No." Cara shook her head. "I haven't. I thought I was, even up until last night, but I was wrong. That was just a crush."

"That was one *big* frigging crush."

Cara laughed, then groaned and rubbed her forehead.

"Yesterday, today." Shan dropped onto a kitchen chair. "What difference does it make? You're in love with him now. I don't see the problem."

Cara stared at her sister. "Michael Finnegan? Super Bowl winning, pro-football star? Hunk extraordinaire?" The verbal list depressed the hell out of her. "I am *so* out of his league. The man's going to break my heart."

"You don't know that."

Meggy snorted. "Cara O'Shea, world famous artist? Make-a-guy's-tongue-drag-on-the-ground body?" She rapped out. "Suck it up, Cara. Besides, I was here last night, and he couldn't keep his eyes off you. I'd say he's in as much trouble as you are when it comes to the L word."

Heat climbed up Cara's chest and to her cheeks. "Lust starts with an L."

Meggy cooed silkily. "And isn't it a fabulous thing?"

She couldn't help but laugh as she returned Meggy's grin. It was too late to do anything about her emotions now. Last night she jumped in with both feet, and the landing was so thrilling she knew she'd repeat the leap if given the chance. She made her bed, literally, she'd just have to lie in it and take whatever came next.

Come to think of it, considering the pleasures she experienced in that bed, she couldn't wait to discover what came next. She barely suppressed a shiver.

"So." Meggy leaned her hips against the counter, a sly smile curving her lips. "Did you take any pictures?"

Meggy ducked when Cara swung out an arm to

smack her upside her head. Laughing, she took a glass from the cabinet, and poured some juice.

"What are you two doing here so early, anyway? Besides trying to catch Finn in his birthday suit."

Shan grinned at Meggy. "I spoke to Mrs. Hawkins yesterday. She's ready to sell us The Palmer House."

Cara turned from popping several pieces of bread into the toaster. "And?"

"We're in, if you're in." Shan's expression turned stubborn as she held Cara's gaze. "A three-way partnership."

Cara pointed at the toaster. "You both know I'm about to burn my breakfast, right?"

Meggy snickered. "Oh, you aren't allowed in the kitchen, unless it's to wash dishes." She grinned at Cara's smirk. "The kitchen is my domain, and Shan's, when she has the time. She'll be handling the personnel and dining room, as well as the business side of things. All *you* have to do is write that big fat check we talked about."

The toast popped up, browned perfectly. Cara grinned at the excellent omen. "I guess I'll get my checkbook."

Chapter Seventeen

Work would be impossible once all the construction began in earnest, so Cara locked herself away with her brushes, giving free reign to the conflicting emotions her father's revelations produced. Three days later, she had four canvases crated to ship to Evan, including the one of her father.

Unforeseen Consequences she titled it.

When she spoke with Evan this morning, she told him about the meeting with her father, filling him in on what she learned about Tom's history with Hannah. His voice heavy with concern, Evan asked if she was okay, if she needed him to come to Palmerton and take her out for a night on the town. She declined, insisting she was fine. He hadn't sounded convinced.

She expected to hear from him again once he received the shipment and he studied the canvases she just signed over to the courier. Evan was much too perceptive of her emotions, especially when he viewed her work. His ability to read a canvas was a little spooky, but that was what made him so good at what he did, and she'd learned to live with it.

Though she had shared some of the darkest secrets of her life with Evan over the years, including the debacle of graduation night, she didn't tell him about her night with Finn. Her feelings for Michael Finnegan were too private to share with a man with whom she'd once been intimate, even if she did consider Evan among her closest friends.

Guilt made her stomach muscles clench. She loved Evan, but he wasn't Finn, so her love for Evan had never progressed beyond that of a friend. And yet, when she needed someone to hold her the night of her first successful show, to help her celebrate her life's dream come true, she had slipped into Evan's arms, finding joy and comfort there.

If she were honest, she could even admit she might have been comfortable sharing a life with him. Their relationship just hadn't worked out that way, thankfully. But if he had pushed to continue their romantic connection, would she have settled for his easy companionship, knowing Finn would never be hers?

Daddy had met and married Ma when he thought a life with Hannah was lost to him. Had Cara acted similarly with Evan? She honestly didn't know, but the similarities in their situations made her feel like a hypocrite.

She pushed aside the uncomfortable insight and grabbed her keys. She was due to pick up Shan's boys at noon, for an afternoon outing.

Jake was beside himself with excitement to be traveling in her new Jeep. With the confidence of a new millennium ten year-old, he programmed and explained the workings of the Bluetooth technology, built into the vehicle, to his technology challenged aunt. By the time they arrived at Cookson Park, he had her cell phone programmed to work with the radio, and God knew what else. She would have to take him for a few more rides before she understood how to use the darn thing.

She cast a solemn glance at the park bench where she met her father a few days earlier, forcing the mood off with a shake when Brian pleaded with her to play Frisbee.

"Okay, punks." She held up the Frisbee. "See if you can catch one."

She let the disk fly, and yelped when it sailed straight up, instead of to where the boys were waiting a dozen yards away. She scrambled out of the way when it came hurtling back to earth, just in time to avoid being conked on the head.

"Okay, punk." Jake leaned over at the waist, laughing. "See if you can *throw* one."

"Smart ass," she grumbled beneath her breath while scooping up the toy. She let out a squeak when a voice spoke very close to her ear.

"Nice language around children, O'Shea."

She spun around and instantly went weak in the knees. *Geez. How pitiful for a grown woman to go all giddy at the sight of a man.* She gobbled Finn up with her eyes, twisting her lips in a cocky grin, and standing still before him, when what she actually wanted to do was shriek, and jump into his arms.

"Stalking again, Finnegan?"

"I'm getting pretty good at it." He wiggled his brows.

She laughed. "You're an idiot."

He grinned and pulled her into his arms for a smacking kiss. "You look delicious, O'Shea."

Thrilled at both his kiss and his words, her heart fluttered at the possibility he suffered the same giddy excitement at seeing her. She relished the moment, absorbing the pleasure of being in his arms, then flustered, she pushed free.

"What are you doing here?"

"Hey, Finn." Jake jogged up to them before Finn could respond.

"Hey, Jake. Brian."

"Why were you kissing Aunt Cara?" Brian came to a stop beside her. He huddled close and stared up at Finn.

Cara wrapped an arm around his thin shoulders, and swung her laughing gaze to meet Finn's.

Finn winked at her before leaning down to prop his hands on his knees. Down on Brian's level, he whispered conspiratorially, "She's awful pretty. I couldn't resist. A man should always try to do the things he likes, don't you think?"

Brian considered that for a moment. "Like playing Frisbee?"

"Like playing Frisbee." Finn straightened, grinning. "Maybe I can help teach your aunt how to throw, so she doesn't give herself a concussion."

Cara shot him a smirk, and he chuckled.

"What's a concussion?"

"It's a broken head." Jake rolled his eyes at his younger brother. "Remember when Davie Jensen crashed his bike into the back of the ice cream truck? He got a concussion."

"Ohhh yeah." Brian drew out the words. He aimed a gap-toothed grin at Finn. "Aunt Cara sucks at throwing the Frisbee. It almost landed on her head."

"Brian!" Cara choked on a horrified laugh.

Finn hooted.

"What?" Brian blinked up at her.

"Don't let your mother hear you using that word. She'll never let you out the door with me again."

"What word?"

Finn snickered, and she jammed him in the ribs with her elbow. He laughed all the harder. She gave up, ruffling Brian's hair. "Never mind, dude."

Jake snatched the Frisbee from her hand, and he and Brian ran off to a safe distance. Jake let the disk fly. Finn caught it clean and sent it back again with a flick of the wrist.

"Show off," she grumbled.

"Hey, I'm a natural athlete."

"Yeah, I heard that somewhere."

He turned to grin at her after tossing the disk to Brian. "Do you want me to teach you how to throw?"

"No thanks." She held out her hand to study her fingers. "I might break a nail."

He chuckled, turning to resume the game. Cara meandered over to sit on a bench in the shade.

She recalled asking Finn the other day if there was anything he couldn't do. Watching him with Shan's boys, she began to believe there wasn't. Why the hell hadn't some smart woman snatched him up? Andrea the Addlepated was a moron.

Finn joined Cara on the bench several minutes later.

"How did the commercial go?"

"It went." He sat back. "I applied their deodorant so many times I'll never have to worry about sweating again. I think my armpits are permanently shellacked." She snorted a laugh, and he chuckled, shrugging. "Hey, it's a living." With his arm behind her, along the top of the bench, he played with a curl from her ponytail.

"How's the staircase look?"

"Oh, Finn, it's gorgeous. I was so excited when they delivered it this morning. I can't wait until it's all done."

"I'll have a crew there at seven in the morning. You'll need to pack a bag for a couple of nights, unless you want to climb a ladder to get in and out of your place. It'll take us at least a day to pull the existing stairwell out, and another to install the spiral. The place will be a mess."

"Oh." She frowned. "I hadn't thought of that."

His wiggled his dark eyebrows suggestively. "When I gave you that tour, did I mention there are sixteen rooms in my house? And did you notice the master bedroom has a king-sized bed?"

She grinned, even as her heart skipped a beat. "Are you inviting me to a sleepover, Finn?"

He twirled a curl around his finger, and his eyes gleamed with lechery.

"Oh, we'll sleep, eventually."

Her body heated, simmering at his words, and the heat in his eyes singed her. Jake called out to them, breaking the connection. Her nephew executed a spinning move that sent the disk flying toward his brother. She resisted the urge to fan herself.

When she glanced at Finn again, the lechery was gone from his eyes, replaced with an odd intensity she couldn't name. He spoke in a low rumble. "I like the idea of you in my bed, of you in my home."

His words should have thrilled her, and would have if not for the slight frown sliding over his brow as though he hadn't meant to say the words, and wasn't pleased he had.

A chill raced down her spine when he dropped the curl he'd been toying with, and pushed a restless hand through his hair. The withdrawal was subtle, but she sensed it, and didn't quite know what to make of it.

She glanced across the park at the boys. "Maybe a sleepover isn't such a good idea."

Finn stared at her, but she didn't turn to meet his gaze. Damn him. *He'd* been the one to suggest she pack a bag and come to his home, not her. *He'd* been the one to call a damn blitz, hounding her until he had her naked and writhing beneath him. She never made a single demand of him, and she'd be dammed if she would take the blame for some imagined slight his football rattled brain had suddenly conjured.

"Why isn't it a good idea? Your place will be a mess and you've got to stay somewhere." Despite his reasonable tone, the wary frown still hovered on his brow when she turned to him.

"Why don't we just forget it? You don't really want me in your home, and I've got several options that will work out fine."

His frown deepened. "What the hell is that supposed to mean? I wouldn't have suggested it if I didn't want you in my home."

She met his gaze calmly. "The frown on your face when you said it says differently. Or are you going to try and tell me you didn't regret making the offer, the moment it came out of your mouth?"

His brows snapped together in offense. He obviously didn't like having the truth pointed out to him. Too bad. She didn't have any experience playing games, while his entire life had been one long, continuous competition. She didn't understand the rules of this particular brand of entertainment and was too intelligent to attempt on-the-job-training while squaring off with a champion.

After a long moment, the frown smoothed out and he sighed. "Look, I'm sorry. It's not what you think. I was thinking of something else and it's my problem, not yours." He cupped her chin and lowered his mouth to drop a gentle kiss on her lips. "No pressure, Cara. It's an open invitation." He checked his watch and stood. "I'm meeting Ryan for a late round of golf and dinner. I need to run."

He turned on his heel.

"Finn." He stopped and glanced over his shoulder. "Finn, I don't..." She held out her hand in supplication, not knowing what to say.

"Like I said, Cara, no pressure. It's just something I'd like." He winked as he walked backwards away from her. "A man should always try to do the things he likes." He spun about, calling a goodbye to the boys, and left the park.

Chapter Eighteen

"He what?" Meggy dropped her sandwich onto her plate.

Cara glanced around the busy Bluebell Diner and kept her voice low. "He asked me to stay with him for a few days while the studio is ripped apart. I think."

"You think? Either he did or he didn't."

"I told you. He made the offer, but I *think* he regretted it immediately. When I called him on it, he said it wasn't what I thought, that he'd been thinking of something else."

"What does that mean?"

"I wouldn't be asking you if I knew." She stabbed a French fry with her fork. "God, men are so confusing."

"Well, what did you say?"

"Are you kidding me? I didn't know what to say, so I just sat there like an idiot and said nothing."

"Well, then. What did he say?"

"He said no pressure. It was just something he'd like."

"Holy crap, Cara. Fabulous Finn the Fine asked you to move in with him."

"No, he didn't. Not like move in, move in. The invitation is just for a few days, until the stairs are done."

"Cara, he's been back in town for four years, and he's watched like a hawk. He doesn't bring any of his women to town, and he's never had a woman in that house. It's off limits to his bimbos. When he's seen with a woman, it's always at his place in Boston. The fact that he asked you to stay with him has to mean something."

Cara snorted. "He's a guy. We're currently having sex. It's a simple matter of convenience."

Meggy chewed a bite of her sandwich, and then shook her head. "He's had sex with a lot of women, but never invited any of them into his home. He has his penthouse lair for that."

Cara set down her fork, her appetite waning. "You're not helping."

"I'm trying to. Someone has to read between the lines in Finn's play book. You're too set on considering yourself the flavor of the week to do it."

"I had it right all those years. The smartest thing to do is steer clear of guys. They're impossible to understand and they know it. They mess with us on purpose to confuse us."

Meggy laughed. "Oh please. The only reason you steered clear of men all those years is because none of them were the oh-so-yummy Finn the Fine."

"I didn't steer clear of all men. Just most of them."

"The hunky art dealer doesn't count. You never even went back for seconds." She laughed at Cara's scowl. "So, what are you going to do?"

Cara picked up her sandwich. "I plan to stay with you tomorrow night."

"Geez, Cara. What am I going to do with you?" Meggy sighed heavily. "Finn the Fine, hunk extraordinaire, invites you to come and play in his playground, even if it's just for a day or two, and you want to sit around watching reruns on the cooking channel with me? Have I taught you nothing?"

Cara smirked, then sighed and shrugged. "I think it would just complicate things."

"And that's a bad thing, because?"

"You know what I mean."

"You're in love with the man, Cara. Playing house for a few days may not be such a bad idea. It might give him some ideas of his own. Like the fact that he likes having you around."

She cocked her head. "For a pain in the butt, you occasionally make a good point."

Meggy smiled, but her attention was focused on the front of the diner. Cara spun around in the booth and stiffened. Hannah Dunn's unhappy gaze met hers from the to-go counter.

Cara wrapped her restless fingers around her water glass as her father's wife shot a nervous glance at the woman three booths away. Cheryl Potter sat with her husband Rick, not bothering to hide her interest in the tableau Cara and Hannah being in the same place presented.

Cara's stomach muscles clenched with nerves as Hannah left the counter. She passed by Cheryl, coming to a stop beside the booth where Cara and Meggy sat.

"Hello, ladies."

"Hannah," Cara murmured.

"Hello, Hannah." Meggy's smile was sharp as she too noticed Cheryl straining her neck in an effort to overhear their conversation. "How have you been?"

Hannah's smile was grateful. "I've been well,

thanks." She looked at Cara. "I hear your studio is coming along."

Cara flicked a glance in Cheryl's direction. The older woman quickly dropped her gaze. "Yes, it is. It's still a mess, with the renovation work that's being done, but it'll be beautiful."

Hannah nodded stiffly and smiled at Meggy. "How are things going with you, Meggy?"

"Fabulous." Her smile was only slightly strained. "Cara, Shan, and I just bought Palmer House."

"Really?" Genuine pleasure lit Hannah's blue eyes. "That's terrific. I didn't know you were interested in opening your own place."

"It's always been in my long range plans. This opportunity just came along at the right time. Shan and I have been experimenting with recipes since we were kids. We love cooking together." She smirked at Cara. "Cara burns toast."

Cara bared her teeth at her friend in lieu of a smile. Hannah laughed softly along with Meggy. "I'll remember that, and come in on the day *you're* cooking." She sent Cara a wary smile.

"That would be pretty much every day." Meggy played with the straw in her glass. "Cara's a silent partner, so you're safe any day you want to come in."

"I'll do that." Hannah fiddled with the strap of her purse as though she didn't know what to do with her hands. "Well, it was nice to see you, girls. Take care."

"You too," Cara and Meggy said together.

Hannah returned to the counter to wait for her order.

"Cheryl Potter is such a cow." Meggy kept her voice low, but she shot daggers at the woman with her eyes. Cheryl sniffed and looked away. "I thought she was going to strain a muscle, trying to overhear what we were saying."

"Which wouldn't have been an issue if Hannah had ignored us." Cara pushed her plate to the side, no longer hungry.

"Maybe that's why she stopped to say hi. She knows you don't like her, and she's not the kind of woman to force an issue. Can you imagine the grapevine tomorrow if the two of you were seen in here tonight, and hadn't spoken to each other? She was just trying to prevent Cheryl from getting an exclusive."

"Well, I'm not going to thank her."

"She's not so bad. I know, I know." Meggy held up a hand before Cara could argue her point. "It's just too bad. She's always been nice to me."

****

Cara had a bag packed and was ready to start work when the crew of six men arrived at seven the next morning. She had set coffee and donuts on the counter. The men drifted over to help themselves before getting started. Finn arched a brow in silent inquiry when he spotted the black duffle bag beside the front door.

She shrugged. "I was invited for a sleepover."

To her relief, he smiled. Lifting the bag, he went outside to stow it in the cab of his truck.

Many hours later, her studio was the mess he had predicted. The work was dirty and dusty. Though the men wouldn't hear of her chipping in with the heavy stuff, she contributed where she could, mostly by fetching tools and drinks, and lunch at noon.

The stairwell was gone and the back wall sported three large openings for the French doors. Heavy plastic sheets hung in their place. The staircase would be installed first thing tomorrow morning. She marveled at the difference she could already see.

Too tired and grimy to be overly self-conscious, she followed along docilely when Finn escorted her inside his home at the end of the day. Though it was possible her exhaustion kept her from noticing any tension on his part, she didn't sense any. Whatever had been bothering him yesterday no longer seemed to be an issue.

He hefted her duffle over his shoulder and guided her up that amazing staircase to the second floor master bedroom. She eyed the king sized bed. Anticipation of the night to come vanquished her fatigue. As though reading her mind, he laughed and dropped her bag on the floor to drag her into the adjoining bathroom and the most decadent shower she'd ever seen.

Eight individually programmed, square showerheads graced the tiled space large enough for four full-sized men to do jumping jacks without getting in each other's way. He snickered at her observation and soon all thoughts of jumping jack men flew from her mind as Finn introduced her to the erotic combination of water, shower gel, and a naked and aroused Finn the Fine.

Two hours later, they lay tangled together in his big bed, discarded Chinese food containers on the night stand. She ran her palm over the exciting expanse of his chest, while his fingers combed through her long curls.

"I love your hair." He twisted a curl around one finger.

"It used to drive my mother crazy." She laughed at the memory. "All those tangled curls needing to be tamed every morning before she'd let me leave for school."

"It's always been long?"

She lifted her head from its place on his shoulder to gaze into his face. "Ma cut it short once. What a disaster." She smiled and let her head drop back on his shoulder. "There are a couple of pictures. I resembled a rabid, red poodle."

His chuckle vibrated through her body where she pressed against him.

"I made a cedar hope chest for one of my cousins a couple of years ago." He tickled her nose with the curl. "It was the same color."

"Ceara."

His hand stilled. "Excuse me?"

"Ceara. It's the Irish form of my name. It means fiery red. My mother is obsessed with all things Irish. She took one look at me in the delivery room the day I was born, and that was that."

"Were you named for your personality, or the color of your hair?" he asked deadpan, and then burst out laughing when she tugged at the hair on his chest in response. "I know Erin comes from Erin go Braugh." He grinned. "Ryan doesn't shut up when he's had a few drinks. You'd be surprised what I know about your sister." She snickered. "It sounds Irish, but where did Shan's name come from?"

"Shannon is the name of a river in southwest Ireland." Absently, she brushed the palm of her hand down his chest, and let her fingers dance across his ribs. "What about you?"

"You can't get much more Irish than Michael Joseph Finnegan, other than putting an O in front of it.

My mother was pure Italian."

"I never met her," she said softly. "I know she passed away shortly before we moved to town and your dad died a couple of years later. That must have been awful. Dad and I may not see eye to eye, but I can't imagine losing either of my parents."

"Yeah." Sighing, he tucked her more closely to his side. "Mom was a pistol. I still miss her. Dad, too. He was never the same after we lost Mom. He went through the motions of living, but he quit caring. I think he was relieved when he got sick. He didn't even try to fight it." Finn went quiet for a moment. "But the family closed ranks and did their best to lessen the loss. Maive made it her mission to act as surrogate mother, and father too, after Dad died."

"Maive." Cara chuckled. "My sisters and I called her the dragon lady. God, she used to scare the crap out of me when I was a kid."

"Just when you were a kid? Most people are still scared of her."

"I happen to like her."

"That's because she let you steal the bookstore away from me."

"Well, there is that," she purred contentedly, and laughed along with him.

"She likes you, too. She's a smart old termagant, I'll give her that. She kept me from veering off the straight and narrow a few times over the years with her unsolicited advice."

"She does give excellent advice." She shrugged when he turned to give her a questioning glance. "I went to see her before I came to apologize." His eyebrows rose in surprise. "I was afraid you'd refuse to do the renovation, even after I said I was sorry."

He lifted on one elbow and gazed down at her. "And Maive helped you out with that?"

She batted her lashes. "A smart woman uses all the weapons at her disposal to stay on top of things."

He didn't have an answer. Instead, he pulled her beneath him, and settled himself between her thighs.

"Then again," she purred as his lips lowered to hers. "Being on the bottom now and then has its rewards, too."

"Shut up, O'Shea," he growled into her mouth.

"Make me." She challenged.

And he did.

Chapter Nineteen

"This looks promising."

Cara gave the Dumpster a dubious glance as Finn swung the car off the dark cobbled street into an alley, nosing the front hood up against discarded crates and boxes. He grinned at her perplexed expression, shutting off the ignition.

He had surprised her when he suggested they go out for a real dinner at a nice restaurant, a change from the meals they'd shared in his bed the last few evenings. She expected him to take her to Spinellis, since it was the nicest restaurant in town. Instead, he pulled out onto the highway and headed south.

The lights of Boston had spread out before them, shimmering reflectively off the water of the bay like a postcard as they crossed the Tobin Bridge. Five minutes later, they exited into old Charlestown, bumping along the narrow, cobblestone streets toward the North End.

A diner's Mecca, if Italian food was on the agenda, the streets of the North End teemed with activity. Pedestrians crowded the sidewalks of Boston's oldest neighborhood beneath antique streetlamps. Part of the Freedom Trail, along with points of interest like The Old North Church and Paul Revere's home, the historic district boasted more Italian restaurants per square inch than anywhere on earth, outside of Italy.

147

"Is this a legal parking space?" She climbed out of his low-slung Jaguar and stood, glancing around.

"I called ahead." He led her to the back door of the early nineteenth century brick building. "Antonio lets me park here and slip in the back. It keeps the vultures at bay."

"Vultures?"

"The press," he replied absently. They entered a kitchen swarming with activity and heavenly scents. He moved behind a tiny gray haired woman, nearly as wide as she was tall, working at one of the stoves. He bent to press a kiss to her cheek. "Hello, Marta. How's my best girl?"

She jumped and turned. A smile spread over her moon shaped face. "Finn! Antonio said you were coming in tonight."

"I needed a manicotti fix."

Her smile widened. "I thought so. Tonight, it's the special."

Across the room at a long, stainless steel table, a short, frail-looking bald man in a food-stained apron glanced up. Below an incredibly thick, snow-white mustache, his mouth broke into a broad smile that wiped any hint of fragility from his bony face.

"Benvenuto, Super Bowl! Welcome." He skirted the table to greet Finn in a heavy Italian accent. Finn shook his hand and returned his smile.

"Antonio, you're looking fit."

The older man laughed. Bushy white brows wriggled above dark chocolate eyes. He slid a sly smile toward Marta.

"My wife, she tells me this every night when I come to her bed."

Finn laughed as Marta rolled her eyes. "Cara, this is Marta. She makes a mean cannoli, and this ugly short-order cook is Antonio Giordano."

"Short-order cook." Antonio snorted, mumbling in Italian. He tossed Finn a smirk, and focused sparkling brown eyes on Cara. "Cara, the beloved," he murmured the Italian translation of her name. "Welcome to Giordano's."

Cara included Marta in her greeting smile. "It's nice to meet you, Mr. and Mrs. Giordano."

He harrumphed. "Antonio, please. Now, tell me why you waste your time on this overgrown Irishman." He jerked his head toward Finn. "A woman as beautiful as you needs a nice Italian boy."

Finn grinned and crossed his arms. "I'm sure Cara's mother, Mary *O'Shea*, would be interested to hear that."

"I tease."

Cara was charmed by the faint blush spreading over Antonio's cheeks.

Marta shook her head. "Pay him no mind, Cara. He longs for grandbabies. So far, our three sons are uncooperative when it comes to marriage."

"My mother would understand completely. She's not averse to demanding a few more grandkids." She grinned. "A nice Italian boy, huh?"

Finn cleared his throat. Antonio laughed and gestured toward the kitchen door, leading them to the dining room, to see them seated at a booth at the back. "I save the best table for you. You'll want Marta's manicotti tonight, no?"

"And a bottle of that red I like."

Antonio nodded and left Cara and Finn alone.

"You're a regular?"

"I've been coming here off and on since college. Antonio's a bit of a gambler. He won a bundle the year we took the Super Bowl." He grinned. "I've been one of his favorites ever since. When you taste Marta's manicotti, you'll understand why I keep coming back."

He relaxed against the bench seat and smiled across at her. The waiter arrived, and she folded her napkin across her lap as he presented the wine. Finn approved the selection and when the wine was poured, he clicked his glass to hers. She hummed her appreciation of the sumptuous merlot.

"Meggy and I used to come to the North End for The Feast every summer. She'd drag me around while she tried to sweet talk the locals into sharing their recipes."

The Feast of St. Anthony had been a tradition in Boston for just short of a century. Thousands of the faithful returned every year for the pageantry of the parades, and to say a prayer and ask a favor at the feet of the statue of St. Anthony of Padua. Cara figured most of the rushing crowds were there for the incredible food.

"How long have you and Meggy been friends?"

She waited while the waiter delivered their plates. "I met her several weeks after we moved into town. She was my first friend in Palmerton."

"She scares the hell out of me," he said with a mock shudder. "She had the town council shaking in their boots last year when they were holding up some money for the girl's athletic program at the high school."

Cara laughed. "That's Meggy. She takes no

prisoners." She scooped a bite of pasta and cheese on her fork and hummed in appreciation. Finn hadn't exaggerated. Marta's manicotti was the best she'd ever experienced. "I don't know what I would have done without Meggy's friendship over the years. She was as much a bodyguard as a friend, back when I was too shy to slap down the cretins."

His blue eyes danced with humor and his fork stalled over his plate. "The cretins?"

Cara offered a self-deprecating smile. "I wasn't very popular with the boys in high school."

He lowered his fork to his plate, his eyes riveted on her face. He shook his head. "I don't know how to tell you this, O'Shea, but your looks would make you popular with *any* high school boy. Believe me, I know. I used to be one."

She laughed. "Oh, I generated a lot of interest, but being taller than most of the boys and having a centerfold body is a curse when you're painfully shy. I used to freeze up when people talked to me, and since most of the interest that came my way from boys scared me, I learned to ignore them. I got a reputation for being stuck up." Her eyes glittered with satisfaction as she recalled one particular high school encounter. "Giving one of my worst tormentors a black eye junior year didn't help my reputation."

"You gave a boy a black eye?"

"I knocked him on his ass," she said with relish, and he laughed.

"A centerfold body with a killer instinct." His eyes twinkled as he considered the combination. "I think I'm in love."

She snorted at his wicked smile, even as her heart

gave a little thump at his words. Playing house with him, as Meggy suggested, had been like living a dream, but Cara had been afraid *she* was the only one getting ideas. Oh, she didn't consider his comment a declaration of love, but the staircase had been completed two days ago and he hadn't said a word about her returning to her apartment. True, the French doors were yet to be installed, but the gaping holes were covered with a temporary wall of plywood. She could move back in anytime. This *thing* between them had begun to feel more like a relationship than a fling. Her heart soared at the possibility he thought so too.

They enjoyed a quiet hour, with Antonio showing up beside their table once their meals were served, to assure his special guests had everything they needed.

Finally, she set down her fork with a groan. "I can't eat another bite." She laughed when Finn pulled the plate of chocolate drizzled cannoli from the center of the table and proceeded to polish it off in three generous forkfuls.

After signing the check, he stood and held out his hand. She placed hers in his, and rose. The flash of a camera temporarily blinded her, and she blinked. Finn shifted until she was standing slightly behind him, and turned to face a short, thirty-something man with flyaway blond curls and intense gray eyes. The expensive camera strung around his neck ruined his guise of hungry tourist.

"No pictures, Stockwell." Though she couldn't see Finn's face, anger was evident in his sharp tone.

"Come on, Finn. Who's the new girl?" Stockwell brought the camera to his eye once again.

Finn laid his free hand on the man's arm, ruining

his aim. Finn's voice was quiet and clipped. "I'd appreciate it if you'd delete that shot."

The photographer quirked his lips in a cynical smile. "Just doing my job."

"I'll give you a heads up the next time there's something to see at the penthouse. Lose the picture," Finn said coldly.

She stiffened. His promise of a scoop involving some future woman brought the reality of their relationship into focus like a cruel slap. Her gaze darted around the hushed room, suddenly aware of the avid interest of the other diners.

Stockwell's calculating stare slid to what he could see of Cara. "I'll hold you to that," he said after a moment's hesitation.

"What's this?" Antonio arrived and pointed a thin finger at the photographer. "You wait outside if you want a table."

With a salute to the angry proprietor, Stockwell strolled out the front door without another word.

"I apologize, my friend. He slipped past us."

Finn clapped a hand on Antonio's shoulder. "It's not your fault, Antonio. Stockwell is persistent. No harm done."

Antonio turned to Cara. "I'm sorry, bella. The press, they haunt our Finn."

A weak smile was about all she could muster.

Antonio escorted them through the kitchen to the back door. Finn shook his hand. "Tell Marta she outdid herself." Without a word, he guided Cara outside and bundled her into the car.

Chapter Twenty

Furious, as much with himself as the greedy freelance photographer, Finn's knuckles showed white from his crushing grip on the steering wheel. He knew only too well the kind of firestorm a woman would face, being seen with him, but he had ignored his own instincts, because he wanted Cara near.

With Stockwell on her scent, the smart thing to do would be to send her home, tonight. But damn it, he wasn't nearly ready to give her up yet. He didn't plan to have a future with her, any more than he had with any of the other women he'd held and let go since his divorce, but for reasons he didn't want to consider, he didn't like the idea of Cara joining the ranks of those other women. And she would, if her picture turned up in one of Stockwell's journalistic rags.

The chances were fifty-fifty the ambitious photographer would hold back the picture he'd snapped. Finn could only hope the promise of a future exclusive would tip the scales.

"Sorry about that. Stockwell is a piranha, but he's backed off in the past when I've asked him to. Hopefully, he'll do the same this time."

She snorted a laugh. "I think that's a safe bet. He could barely contain his excitement at your offer of an exclusive. The question is...how long will you make him wait?"

He jerked his head in her direction, but she was staring out the side window so he couldn't see her face. Though she had no qualm voicing her disdain of his lifestyle before they became lovers, she hadn't made reference to his reputation since they'd been sleeping together. He didn't like hearing her do so now.

"I like women, Cara," he said stiffly. "There have been a lot of them since my divorce. It's who I am, and I won't apologize for it."

"I didn't ask for an apology." She glanced at him, her big, green eyes full of disappointment. She laughed, a short and humorless cough. "I went into this affair with my eyes wide open. You don't owe me any explanations, and I certainly don't expect any."

"Jesus." He flexed his cramping fingers on the wheel. "I'm sorry. Dealing with the press always puts me in a vicious mood."

"I can see that," she said, her voice now as stiff as his.

"It pisses me off that I can't just flatten an asshole like Stockwell when he gets in my face."

"Then why offer him an exclusive? And that's not a criticism. I'm just trying to understand. Why reward him for hounding you, when that will only encourage him to continue?"

"First, because nothing I do or say is going to stop him. To bottom feeders like Stockwell, celebrities are a multimillion-dollar business, and they take their job seriously. Feeding them information on my terms allows me to have at least a little bit of control over what's being reported. And second, though it ticks me off to admit it, the paparazzi have their uses. Having my name and face in the public eye increases my interest quotient, or so my agent tells me. When you make your living as a pitch man, the publicity comes in handy at the bargaining table."

"That sounds like a crappy way to make a living." She turned back to the window. "It must drive you crazy sometimes."

"You have no idea."

****

"Word on the town grapevine is, Cara O'Shea has moved into the Sawyer House."

Finn closed the cover on the electrical panel and shot Maive an aggravated frown where she perched on her basement stairs. "She hasn't moved in. She just needed somewhere to stay while we replaced the stairwell in her studio."

"Would that be the stairwell you finished over a week ago?"

He squatted to close the toolbox at his feet. "What is it you're driving at, Maive?"

"I'm not driving at anything, boy. I'm asking flat out. What are you up to with Mary O'Shea's middle daughter?"

"Since when do you ask questions about my love life?"

"Since you've invited a woman into your home for the first time since Andrea."

"Don't make more of it than it is."

"And what is that?"

"A temporary arrangement between two consenting adults." He snapped the latches on the box and hefted it as he stood. Maive rose as he reached the bottom step, blocking his way.

"It's me you're talking to, Michael Finnegan. Since Andrea, you haven't let a woman get close long enough to have even a temporary arrangement, until Cara. I like her."

He sighed and shook his head. "I like her, too. What's not to like? But don't go spinning dreams of happily-ever-after. You'll only be disappointed. Neither of us wants anything permanent. We're simply two healthy adults, enjoying each other's company for a time."

Perplexity marred her brow. "Why don't you want something permanent? She's perfect for you, and I've seen the way you look at her. She has feeling for you, too."

He grunted, recalling the acceptance in Cara's eyes when she named what they were doing together, an affair. She couldn't have made it any clearer she considered their relationship temporary. She may care for him. Her eyes said so, as did the way she responded whenever he reached for her, but she was smart enough to know their relationship wouldn't last. Her insight should have relieved him. Instead, it left him feeling itchy.

"Maive." He sighed and moved to step passed her. She stuck out her arm, stopping him.

"Don't Maive me, boy. Just answer the question."

"Maive darling, you know I love you, but you're seeing things that aren't there. Besides, we both know I don't have what it takes to make a relationship work."

"Poppycock!"

He barked a laugh. "Poppycock?"

She ignored his grin, pointing a finger in his face. "Andrea was the one who didn't have what it takes. If she hadn't left, you'd still be there, doing everything you could to make your marriage work. And you'd be miserable. When are you going to stop blaming yourself for her selfishness?"

The grin slid from his face. "You're biased, Auntie Maive. It took two of us to screw up our marriage. I knew the kind of life she expected to live when I married her. When I was injured, I quit trying to give her the life I had promised."

Her face softened and she cupped his cheek with a gentle hand. "And she didn't love you enough to give you the time to work through your own disappointment at never playing football again. She was a selfish woman, more concerned about being seen about town than she was about what you were going through. You're better off without her."

All true, but still only half the story. He'd been so caught up in his own nightmare he didn't noticed how unhappy Andrea was until it was too late. Maybe he hadn't loved *her* enough to notice.

"I love you, Maive." He lifted her hand and pressed a kiss to her palm before using his grip to turn her and guide her up the stairs. "And like I said, you're biased."

"Cara, on the other hand is just the kind of woman you need." She continued as though he hadn't spoken. "She's strong enough to stand up to you, but human enough to make you happy." She spun around at the top threshold, her eyes even with his when he stopped several steps below. "I promised your mother I'd watch out for you. I've tried to do that."

"You've succeeded." He squeezed her hand before letting go. "You've always been there for me."

"Yes, I have, even when you resented it."

His mouth kicked up in a crooked smile. He'd tested his budding manhood against her indomitable will more than once. She'd been as tough as any coach he ever played under and she had usually been right.

"But the one time you really needed me to be there for you, I wasn't." She shook her head when he would have argued and moved aside so he could join her in the hallway. "I didn't speak up when you told me you were marrying Andrea. I should have. I won't make that mistake again." She poked him in the chest with a gnarled finger. "Cara O'Shea is perfect for you, boy. Don't screw it up!"

Chapter Twenty-One

"It's an important celebration, Finn. The anniversary committee has been waiting for your answer for weeks now. You can't keep dodging us."

Despite her agitation, Jill Carlson appeared fresh and crisp in a pale peach business suit. Her perfectly styled hair flitted about her shoulders as she followed Finn around the studio.

Cara chewed on her bottom lip, and remained silent. In contrast, Finn was hot and sweaty in his ripped T-shirt and jeans. Crouched beside one of the new French doors, his narrowed eyes warned he was considering using the hammer he held to clobber the Palmerton anniversary committee chairwoman on the head.

"Palmerton is my home, Jill. Keeping my name out of functions and events here keeps the press away."

"Exactly," she persisted, ignoring his valid point and settling on emotional blackmail. "Palmerton is your home, and you owe it to the people of this town, who supported you in your career, to step up to the plate for this celebration."

He answered her with a silent, sardonic arch of his brows.

"We need you." Her New England accent deepened with her whining tone. "The two-hundred-fiftieth anniversary of incorporation only comes along once."

"There are plenty of others who would be happy to take the position." Finn pounded away at the shim he was attempting to install to level the French door's threshold. "Tom O'Shea is the town manager. Ask him."

"He's the one who suggested you!" Despite her bulldog tactics, Jill was genuinely interested in the senior center the celebration would help to fund. Finn's presence would draw the kind of crowds the committee was hoping for, if only she could talk him into it. Her eyes pleaded with Cara. "Can't you talk to him?"

"Leave me out of this." Cara held up a hand. "I've only been in town for a few weeks. I don't have a dog in this hunt."

"Don't have a dog in this hunt?" Jill stared at her as though she'd lost her mind. "You're a resident of this town too, and you're *sleeping* with him! If anyone can talk some sense into him, it's you!"

Struggling with her own shock, Cara barely noticed the sounds of construction go silent, until one of the men groaned behind her. Beside her, Finn rose slowly from his crouch. Six-foot-five, two hundred and twenty pounds of muscled menace turned on Jill.

"Oooh, nooo." Jill breathed shallowly and paled.

"Oh, no, is right!" His voice rose until the last word was a shout.

Cara stepped between them to pull the hammer from his hand before he decided to put it to good use. She turned on a horrified Jill.

"You're right, Jill." She crossed her arms, the hammer dangling from her gripping fingers. She was amazed her voice sounded so calm, considering the town crier had just announced her sexual escapades to a half dozen men. "I am sleeping with him, but unlike you, I'm only using him for sex, not to put Palmerton on the map."

Ryan burst out laughing behind her. Several of the other men snickered. That is, until Finn jerked his furious gaze in their direction. A round of nervous coughing ensued.

Tears filled Jill's eyes. "God, I'm sorry, Cara." She turned to Finn. "I'm sorry, Finn. I never should have said that."

"No, you shouldn't." He stomped over to the water cooler and filled a paper cup, draining it without taking a breath.

The damage done, Cara attempted to diffuse the tension, despite her own embarrassment. "Why can't you find someone else to be the grand marshal? Finn obviously doesn't want to do it."

"There is no one else. Everyone wants Finn to do it. He's just concerned about the potential chaos because of the press he'll draw. But we've already addressed that problem." Jill shifted into sales mode once more. "We'll have a press tent beside the viewing stand for the parade. He'll only have to make a brief statement and answer a few questions."

He snorted rudely, but Jill continued "We've already set up a four-man subcommittee to deal with the press, Finn. If they want a spot at the press conference, they'll have to abide by our rule that you be left alone."

"The press makes their own rules." He tossed his empty cup in the trash pail, turning an angry glare on the workers who were following the conversation with interest.

Ryan cleared his throat. "I think it's time for a lunch break. Come on, guys." Finn tossed him an appreciative smile as the men filed out through one of the open French doors.

Before Finn could speak, Cara interjected. "Is the press the only reason you don't want to do it?"

His lips thinned with displeasure. "Isn't that enough?"

She had a taste of his disdain for certain members of the press at dinner the other night, and yet *he* had pointed out they also had their uses.

"If anyone knows how to work the press, Finnegan, it's you. Besides, the attention wouldn't hurt the fund raiser for the senior citizens center, and your involvement will up the *interest quotient*." He glared at her, hearing his own words coming back at him. She refused to be intimidated. "That *was* the reason the committee decided to combine the fund raiser with the celebration in the first place, wasn't it?"

At his darkening scowl, Jill shifted toward the front of the room. "I'll talk to you about this later. I forgot I had another appointment."

When the door banged shut, Finn lurched forward and wrenched the hammer from her loosened grip. He pointed it at her, handle first, leaning in until they were almost nose to nose.

"Using me for sex doesn't give you the right to stick your nose in my Goddammed business!"

She stumbled back as though he had slapped her. After the incident with Stockwell last week, and the contentious conversation that followed, she expected

Finn to make some excuse to end their affair or least send her packing. He hadn't, and she began to believe she wasn't alone in her belief that they had something lasting. Having him reconfirm the temporary nature of their relationship made her want to cry, but she couldn't blame him for being angry. He'd told her what he thought of the press. She should have stayed out of it. And she shouldn't have said what she did to Jill, either.

She heaved a weary breath. "You're right. I shouldn't have interfered. I won't again. And I'm sorry for the *using you for sex* comment. Jill pissed me off, and I wasn't thinking." She tossed the shim she held onto the counter. "I think I'll call it a day."

****

Finn watched Cara climb the stairs to her apartment and barely stopped himself from hurling the hammer through the glass of one of her new doors. The hurt in her eyes when she offered her apology stung like a raw wound. He cursed himself for putting it there, but damn it. Why couldn't women just enjoy an affair for what it was, without involving themselves in every other area of a man's life?

Afternoon stubble scratched at the palm he rubbed over his face. He should have followed his instincts the night they met up with Stockwell, and walked away from her then. Each day their affair continued, their relationship became more and more complicated, for both of them.

His gaze followed the curve of her prized spiral staircase to the apartment door at the top of the landing. Their argument was the perfect excuse to put an end to a relationship he would screw up eventually. But instead of climbing those stairs and doing what needed to be done, he pulled the cell phone from his pocket and punched Jill's number.

"I'll ride in the damn lead car," he growled when she picked up. "But don't come crying to me when your quaint little celebration turns into a circus, because I'll just say, I told you so!"

****

The week leading up to the anniversary celebration passed swiftly for Cara. With Finn's promise to act as grand marshal, volunteers spruced up Cooksen Park where the viewing stand would be located. The Blue Bell diner did a brisk business, supplying lunch for the workers. Merchants decorated their storefronts, while town workers swept and scrubbed the curbs. The citizens of Palmerton were abuzz with excitement over the town's big day.

Finn adamantly refused to discuss the celebration. He'd be the grand marshal, fulfilling his obligation to the town that had supported him his whole life, but he damned well didn't want to know anything more about it. Just tell him what time to show up, he had said. He would make his speech and ride in whatever car they pointed him toward.

Though Cara wished she could blame her imagination, she sensed a change in him. He did nothing she could point to conclusively, as if to say, aha, that's it! That's the kind of thing making me sense a cooling of your interest. And yet, she couldn't shake the feeling his interest had cooled somehow.

He still talked with her and made her laugh while they worked to finish the studio with his crew, or in the evenings when they were alone. He certainly hadn't pulled away when it came to their physical relationship.

There was no question he still wanted her, not when he took every opportunity to see she wanted him, too. When they were in lying in bed, wrapped in each other's arms, he never wore the haunted expression she had seen in his eyes once or twice, when he didn't know she was looking.

She moved back into her apartment the day after Jill's visit. With the stairs and doors installed, she decided she shouldn't overstay her welcome. He'd invited her for a couple of nights, and those nights had stretched into several weeks. He didn't argue when she told him she was going home, but when work on the studio was done each day, he climbed the stairs behind her. He had spent every night since in her bed.

Work continued to progress on her studio with thrilling results. With only finish work left to do, Bob Burns and Finn were the only ones left working on Friday morning when the front door opened.

"Evan!" Cara squealed, running across the expanse of the studio to launch herself at her friend. He swung her in his arms before setting her back on her feet. She returned his grin. "What are you doing here?"

"I wanted to see this amazing studio you've been gushing about." His dubious gaze scanned the clutter of construction tools. "I guess it's a work in progress."

She followed his gaze to the back wall of the building and settled on Finn. She frowned slightly at the closed stare on his face where he crouched, sealing the threshold of the last door.

"You should have seen it a couple of days ago. The new staircase is in, and we're just finishing the French doors. Isn't it fabulous?" Linking her arm through Evan's, she pulled him toward the back of the room.

"Come on. There's someone I want you to meet."

Finn rose as they approached.

"Finn. This is my friend and agent, Evan Malone. Evan, Michael Finnegan."

Evan nodded and stuck out his hand. Finn wiped his palm across his dusty T-shirt before shaking Evan's hand. A wrinkle of confusion marred Evan's brow beneath his wheat colored hair.

"Nice to meet you. I was at the Giants game five years ago when you drilled that pass into the end zone to steal the game, and our playoff hopes, with two seconds left."

"Mullen made a great catch." Finn shrugged his broad shoulders and gave the credit to his favorite tight-end.

Evan's gaze flicked to Cara before returning to Finn. "I never would have expected to find an all-pro quarterback installing hardware, but then, when Cara is involved, nothing surprises me."

Cara rolled her eyes. "Finn is my contractor. The finished woodwork you see around here is his work."

Evan's golden brown eyes passed over the woodwork. "I'm impressed."

"So was I." Cara smiled softly at Finn. "I browbeat him until he agreed to help me get this place into shape."

He didn't respond to her gentle teasing as she expected. Instead, he spoke in a clipped tone. "We're about done for today." He slipped the hammer into the belt at his waist, his focus dropping to her fingers, still wrapped around Evan's arm, before his eyes rose to meet hers. "We'll be back in the morning to clean up and finish. You'll have your studio in working shape by the time the anniversary celebration begins, but the floors will still be tacky, so I wouldn't suggest throwing open your doors to the mob."

"Anniversary celebration?" Evan glanced between them.

"The town turns two hundred fifty tomorrow." Distracted, she spoke to Evan without glancing away from Finn. He'd made it clear he didn't want anything to do with tomorrow's festivities, but she thought he had put his anger behind him. "This is my private studio, Finn. I hadn't planned on opening it to the public, tomorrow or any other day."

He responded with a neutral grunt.

Evan patted her hand resting on his arm and smiled down into her face. "If the pieces she's already shipped to me are an indication of the type of work this place inspires, then I say any investment she's made will be well worth it."

"We aim to please." Finn bared his teeth in a smile that didn't reach his eyes. Bob Burns called down to him from the landing above, interrupting them. Finn left to climb the stairs with a muttered, "Excuse me."

"You liked the canvases?" she asked Evan as she followed Finn's progress up the stairs.

"I've already had an offer on *Unforeseen Consequences*. Do you want to talk about it?"

She knew he was talking about the painting, and not the offer, but she was still just as confused as she'd been that afternoon when she finally spoke to her father. Finn's perplexing moodiness forgotten for the moment, she leaned her head against Evan's shoulder. "No, I don't. I've missed you, Evan."

Evan's gaze lifted to Finn as he descended the

stairs and began gathering up tools for the day. When he glanced back at her, his smile was dubious.

"From the looks of things around here, you haven't had time to miss me."

"I have been a little busy." She cursed the blush heating her cheeks.

"Have dinner with me," he said suddenly. "I'm in town to meet with an artist in the Back Bay." He twisted his wrist to check his watch. "I'll be an hour, but free the rest of the evening."

"Seven sharp, tomorrow," Finn called out as he and Bob passed by. "We'll be resealing the hardwood first thing, so find somewhere to store your stuff."

He bent to heft a circular saw before heading for the door.

"Cara." Evan drew her attention though her eyes stayed on Finn. "Shall I wait, or will you meet me downtown?"

"I'll meet you. Where?"

"I'm at the Four Seasons." Curling a finger under her chin, he turned her until he could drop a kiss on her mouth. "Eight o'clock good for you?" She nodded. His gaze cut to the door and Finn. "It was good to meet you, Finn."

"Same here." Finn shut the door behind him with a thud.

Evan rounded on her. "*Michael Finnegan* is your contractor?"

"It's a long story." She stared at the closed door with her heart pounding in her chest. He seemed so angry. Could he be jealous? Jealous of Evan? The possibility sent a tickling thrill up her spine.

"I'm sure it is." Evan checked his watch. "I've got

a few minutes. Let's hear it."

Her smile was wide with giddy excitement. Laughing, she wrapped her arms around him and pressed a smacking kiss to his cheek. "I really have missed you, Evan."

****

Finn yanked the saw from the bed of the pickup with restrained violence. He'd recognized that man's type the moment Evan Malone stepped through the door. The thousand-dollar, oatmeal colored suit screamed money, while the lean build and patrician appearance whispered sophistication. He'd added predator to his mental list of adjectives describing Cara's agent when he glared into Evan Malone's golden brown eyes. The man was no harmless trust fund playboy.

He now knew the identity of Cara's one and only other lover. He hadn't needed to see Cara throw herself into the man's arms to know they shared more than simple friendship. Malone didn't look at her with the eyes of a friend. His were the eyes of a man who had tasted her sweetness and thirsted for more. The vision of the handsome agent pressing a kiss to Cara's mouth burned on the screen of Finn's mind, and he did his best to ignore the surge of jealousy blasting through him.

He had no business getting bent out of shape. He had no claim on her, and it was only a matter of time when he'd have no contact with her either, other than that of neighbor. They'd be living in the same town, and a woman who looked the way she did...Well, he'd better get used to seeing her with other men.

The idea made him want to rip something apart, or someone. He fought the overwhelming urge to drive back over to her studio and snatch her away from her *friend*. He'd let Malone know in no uncertain terms that Cara O'Shea was his.

Unfortunately, that was a lie. This relationship between them wouldn't last. It was time he accepted that truth. He slammed the tailgate on the truck and carried the saw inside.

Chapter Twenty-Two

Cara climbed the steps of the library wearing a sappy smile. Jealous! A warm flame sparked in her belly. Finn had nothing to be jealous about, and she'd explain that to him, but in the meantime, she couldn't help being thrilled at the possibility he might care more than he let on.

He may not be in love with her, but he cared, and caring could develop into love, with a little time. She was no longer a shy kid, afraid to speak up and cause a scene. She loved Michael Finnegan with all her heart and she wanted more than just a short term affair. It was time she told him.

And if hearing she loved him sent him running? Well, then...she'd just have to kill him.

She hummed as she opened the library doors. The building would be closing for the night in just a few minutes, so she hurried to the romance section to select a book to replace the one she returned. Maybe she'd find something she could read aloud to Finn.

She shook her head and grinned. A month with Finn the Fine and she had turned into a shameless hussy!

Her grin faded when she recognized the quiet voice of a woman two rows away in the young adult aisle. Cara's fingers gripped the binding of the paperback she pulled from the shelf. Meggy had mentioned Hannah volunteered at the library two afternoons a week, but Cara had forgotten.

"Here it is," she heard Hannah say. "It's a true story. I think you'll find it has some similarities with your own."

"Have you read it?" a young voice asked.

"Yes, I have. It's well written and covers some of the struggles and emotions that come with discovering you're adopted."

"Were you adopted?"

"No, I wasn't."

The girl was quiet for a moment. "Were you a birth mother? I want to meet mine eventually."

Cara stood paralyzed between the shelves of books. She held her breath, waiting for Hannah to deny the question.

"I gave up a child for adoption, yes. She was placed with a wonderful family, just as you were. I'm sure your birth mother would be thrilled to know how happy you are with your adoptive family."

Cara couldn't breathe. Abandoning the book she'd selected, she slipped down the aisle between towering shelves and rushed passed the counter at the front of the library. She shoved open the double glass doors. Gulping air like a landed fish, she staggered out into the early evening sunlight, scrambling down the steps to the parking lot and her vehicle. Her hands shook, and she fumbled with the lock before climbing inside.

Pulling the truck door closed behind her, she rested her forehead on the steering wheel. Horrifying possibilities thundered in her head. Hannah had given up a child for adoption? Oh God, Daddy! Had the child been his? Did he know about it?

How long Cara sat there, running the possibilities through her head, she didn't know. The beep of her cell phone, signaling a text message, interrupted the fury of questions scrambling her brain. She glanced through the window, ignoring the message. Her hands clenched on the steering wheel at seeing Hannah exiting the library to walk to her own car. Cara sat forward and fought with the keys until she found the right one. She shoved the key into the ignition and twisted. Shifting the Jeep into drive, she pulled from the parking lot.

A block away, Hannah swung into a parking space in front of her father's accounting agency and went inside. Cara searched for an empty spot, finding one three doors down. She parked, jumped from her vehicle, and on shaking legs, hurried through the front door of her father's office.

Tom sat at his big desk, visible through the open door. He glanced up when Cara entered, a surprised smile lighting his face. A moment later, the smile evaporated. He jumped to his feet and walked around his desk.

"What's happened? Is it Mary?"

"Tom?" Hannah emerged from the back room with a stack of files in her arms. She stumbled to a stop when she spotted Cara.

"What's the matter, Cara?" Tom repeated, exiting his office.

Cara only had eyes for Hannah. "You had a child?"

Files flew and scattered on the floor at Hannah's feet. Her hands flew to her mouth to cover the cry she didn't quite prevent. Her frantic gaze jerked to Tom's, whose face went as pale as his wife's.

"Let's go in my office, Cara."

Cara ignored him, intent on getting an answer from Hannah. "You had a child you gave up for adoption? I was in the library. I heard you!"

"That's enough, Cara." Tom reached for her arm. She stumbled back, avoiding his touch.

"No, it's not enough, Daddy. You wanted me to know what happened. Well, I'm asking for an explanation now. Did you..." She stopped to catch her sobbing breath. "Oh, God. Did you have a child you put up for adoption or not?"

Tears dripped down Hannah's cheeks. Cara's knees buckled. She locked them tight as Tom slipped his arm around Hannah's shoulders and hugged her protectively to his side. He turned haunted eyes on Cara. "Hannah was pregnant when her family sent her away."

Cara moaned at the affirmation and shuffled backward until the back of her knees made contact with the waiting room couch. She dropped onto it.

Hannah slumped against the desk with her face in her hands while Tom crouched down in front of Cara.

"They took Hannah away, Cara. And when the baby was born, they took her away, too. She was given to a private adoption lawyer to be placed with a family here in the states."

"Her?" Cara's croak was barely audible.

Unshed tears shimmered in his eyes. "We had a daughter, Cara. And they stole her from us."

She glanced over his shoulder. Hannah's face was pale and damp with tears. "Why did you come to Palmerton, Hannah?"

Hannah raised her chin. "I came to be near my daughter."

"She's here?" Cara cried. "She's here in Palmerton?" Her eyes flew to Tom. "Why didn't you tell us? I have a sister? Shan and Erin." She gulped. "We have a sister somewhere in Palmerton, and you didn't think we would want to know?"

"And what was I supposed to tell you? We assume she doesn't know about us, much less you or your sisters. The situation was complicated enough without involving anyone else."

The adamancy of his claim brought Cara up short. He was right, of course. But, God, she had another sister.

"How did you find her? There are laws surrounding adoption that make it almost impossible for birth parents to find children who haven't initiated contact."

He straightened from his crouch and joined Hannah, who answered Cara's question.

"I never had anything to do with my family after what they did to your father and me. When I reached my twenty-fifth birthday I gained access to my trust fund. I used that money to buy the information."

"And you never contacted her? You just moved here and skulked around the edges of her life?"

"That's enough, Cara." Tom frowned.

Hannah placed a hand on his arm. "She was already seven years old by the time I tracked her down and settled here in Palmerton. Her adoptive parents are good people, and they have done nothing wrong to deserve our interference. There have been enough lives ripped apart because I was too much of a coward to fight my family. I'm content to be able to see her, and to know she's happy."

"Who is she?"

"She hasn't tried to find us, Cara." Tom shoved a weary hand through his hair. "Contacting her now would cause her and her adoptive parents heartache. Haven't we all suffered enough already? Let it go."

The sadness in his voice made Cara's stomach hurt. Her eyes stung with tears as he clutched Hannah's hand as though it were a lifeline. Staggered by the revelations, she could only imagine what it must have been like for them to carry their grief for so many years. Suddenly, she was so tired she could barely move. She forced herself to stand. Walking to her father, she kissed his cheek.

"I'm sorry, Daddy."

He lifted his free hand to cup her cheekbone. "Cara, mine."

Her gaze moved to Hannah. Cara didn't know what to say. So much of her unhappiness had been placed at Hannah's feet, and while Cara couldn't completely forgive either of them for what they had done, she also couldn't blame them or hold on to her anger anymore.

"I'm sorry, Hannah," she whispered, before turning and leaving them alone in their grief.

****

Finn tossed his keys onto the Queen Anne table in the spacious entryway of his Beacon Hill penthouse. The place smelled of emptiness, despite the efforts of the cleaning crew he knew would have been here this morning.

He stopped at the wet bar and poured a tumbler full of whiskey before sliding open the glass door leading to the balcony. Leaning a hip against the wrought iron railing, he sipped at the burning liquid.

Ten flights below, streetlights began to flicker on. Beyond the skyline in the distance, the sun dipped below the horizon, bringing night to Bean Town.

Jamming his fingers through his hair, which should have been trimmed weeks ago, he tried to understand just when his life got so damned screwed up. The underlying despair and desperation he had been living with for far too long hadn't begun with Cara O'Shea's return. His life was a mess long before he walked into Maive's parlor a month earlier. Nor had it begun with Andrea's stunning pronouncement that she no longer loved him and was heading on to more exciting adventures.

The DVD down the hall in the media room documented the exact moment when his life had gone to shit. He had watched the recording so often he could run the clip through his mind even now, without aid of modern technology. The moment he'd taken the freak hit to his knee in the second game of his sixth season in Tampa, his charmed life had come crashing down around him.

He'd been a ball player his entire life, and the second he felt the hit, he knew he would never play again. The one thing he had been able to count on was ripped away in the blink of an eye. Without football, what was left?

Not family. He watched his mother fade away while his father clung desperately to her slender fingers. He then watched his father follow her not long afterward. And certainly not marriage—Andrea proved their marriage a fleeting fantasy when she walked out without a backward glance.

He swallowed another sip, welcoming the burning

in his throat. If he was honest, he couldn't even fault Andrea for skipping out the way she did. He'd been so crushed by the loss of his career, so mired in his own broken dreams, he had shut down. Restless, yet uninterested in what the future held, he simply stopped caring. He was surprised she stayed as long as she had.

She'd probably done him a favor by beating him to the punch. The direct hit to his ego finally pulled him out of his lethargy, at least on a basic level. The only real relief he knew from the demon of restlessness that had taken over his charmed life, had been the constant flow of women, but even that faded over time.

He'd filled his life with women, travel, and sponsorships, always moving on to the next challenge before the current one fell apart. He made more money than he could spend in two lifetimes, but he hadn't been truly happy since the moment his opponent's shoulder connected with his knee.

The only real pleasure he had found, in more years than he wanted to count, was when he worked with the kids at the day camp eight weeks each summer, or when building something with his hands. And spending time with Cara. He would screw that up before long, too.

He'd fallen in love with her—a damn stupid thing to do, and there was a good possibility she loved him as well. The stark emotion in her expressive eyes the night they first made love was impossible to miss.

He should have walked away from her then. He should have shouted at her to find a man, a whole man, one who could love her back the way she deserved. She needed a man who wouldn't cut and run before the love and trust died in her eyes, and killed what was left of his soul.

A man like Evan Malone.

Finn checked his watch. Eight-fifteen. She'd be with Evan now, in his suite at the Four-Seasons.

Finn wanted to rage at the very idea of Cara O'Shea with another man. Instead, Michael Finnegan, ex-all-pro, Super Bowl winning quarterback, sank to the concrete balcony floor of his exclusive penthouse apartment, dropped his head against his raised knees, and did something he hadn't done since his mother died. He wept.

Chapter Twenty-Three

Cara woke to the pale pink streaks of dawn stabbing like shards of colored glass through the sparkling windows of her bedroom. She blinked against the morning light, eyes scratchy and sore from the tears she shed throughout the night.

Throwing aside the sheet, she stumbled to the bathroom. When she entered the kitchen several minutes later, she grabbed a mug and filled it with coffee, then headed downstairs to finish storing her supplies. Finn would be here in fifteen minutes to seal the floors.

She had no idea what she would to say to him when he arrived. Somehow she didn't think he would appreciate her demanding to know where he had disappeared to the night before. She was mad enough she wouldn't bother asking. It was the principle of the thing. They would however, be discussing the merits of common courtesy. She'd been worried about him, had left several messages on his cell. At the very least, he should have called or sent a text to let her know he was okay.

A knock on the front door made her jump. Finn had a key, so it wouldn't be him. Shoving the last of the supplies onto a shelf, she went to see who was knocking on her door at seven in the morning. Bob

Burns shuffled his feet on the sidewalk outside, his battered baseball cap twisted into a mangled mess in his beefy palms.

"Good morning, Bob." She leaned to one side, glancing beyond him to the quiet street. His old pickup sat alone at the curb.

Following the direction of her gaze, his Adam's apple bobbed in his throat as he swallowed. His hat suffered further damage at the nervous flexing of his fingers.

"It's, ah, just me." He cleared his throat. "I'm here to seal the floor. I'ya, guess Finn had some things he needed to do. He called me to say, that is, he wanted me to..." His customary smile absent, Bob couldn't quite meet her eyes. He stared down at his shoes. "He asked me to come finish it."

She didn't flinch at his choice of words, though she wanted to, but she refused to be embarrassed because Finn chose to involve his friend in his obvious brush off. "Finish it," she murmured. The sudden thumping of her heart caused her head to spin. She forced a deep breath.

"Then I guess you'd better come on in." She swung the door wide.

Between them, Cara and Bob finished sealing the floor by nine. She painted toward the steps leading to her apartment, while Bob worked his way to the front door.

"You should be able to walk on the floor in an hour. Just don't drag anything across it for a while, until it's had plenty of time to cure."

They were the first words either of them had spoken since she let him in the door. She smiled and thanked him for his help. He closed the front door behind him. Cara sat on the bottom landing of her new staircase and stared at her finished studio.

It was a small consolation, but she was glad now that Finn hadn't been home when she fled to his place after leaving her father and Hannah last night. She had her pride, enough that she shriveled inside knowing she had run to a man who decided their affair was over, but didn't have the balls to tell her to her face.

Finn jealous of Evan? What a fool she was. What she expected all along had happened.

Her back stiffened on a spurt of healing anger and she straightened. She'd thought a lot of things about Michael Finnegan over the years, but she never considered him a coward. She did now. His mood of late plainly said he'd rather be somewhere else. Instead of stringing her along and continuing to sleep with her, he should have ended the affair weeks ago.

Her gaze ran over her beautiful, finished studio and she wished she could paint. She needed to paint, but that would have to wait, for now. Pushing to her feet, she went upstairs to get ready for the incorporation celebration.

****

Spruced and polished, downtown Palmerton presented its true identity, a two-hundred-fifty-year-old New England town that had weathered good times and bad. The celebration committee had done themselves proud. Bright, red, white, and blue bunting hung suspended over Center Street along the parade route. The streets were cleaned and the viewing stands assembled.

The press tent swarmed with journalists, all eager

for an interview with the town's most famous citizen. As parade time neared and there was still no sign of Finn, Jill and her band of subcommittee members did their best to keep the peace, promising he would be there soon to make a short speech and answer their questions. The longer they were kept waiting, the less polite the press became in their demands.

Since no one had seen him that morning—Cara had been asked by no less than eighteen people where he was—she figured the shining star of Palmerton was seeing to it his prediction from last week came true. The press tent already resembled a circus.

Cara watched the chaos from behind the information table where she'd been assigned to pass out the brochures the chamber of commerce provided, highlighting the town's history. She balked at the assignment when Jill told her where they wanted her, not wishing to be anywhere near the action when Finn finally showed up to charm the press, if he ever did.

She begged for a position in the children's face painting booth, but was shot down. As a successful artist, the committee wanted her at the press conference. Apparently she was to be a backup attraction at the circus.

Maive sat in a chair next to the table. She stopped by the press tent a few minutes earlier, and proceeded to harass one of the subcommittee members into procuring her a chair so she could watch the press conference in comfort. Cara was handing her a brochure when Jill's clear voice stilled the restless crowd.

"Finally! Ladies and gentlemen, our grand marshal has arrived."

Cara glanced up and spotted the throng moving along the sidewalk toward them. At six-five, Finn's dark head was visible over those of the mob surrounding him. The press proved as unruly as Finn predicted. They surged forward to intercept him. Their questions flew like bullets.

"How does it feel to be honored in your home town? Any new endorsement contracts, Finn? Any plans to coach?"

"Ladies and gentlemen, if you'd give him a little room, I'm sure Finn will be happy to answer all your questions." Jill's no nonsense voice caused a lull, and Maive took advantage.

"All of you vultures move on back, so I can see my grandnephew."

Cara stared in amazement as, like the Moses of Palmerton, Maive's spoken demand parted the crowd like the Red Sea. One by one, the members of the press shuffled to the side, leaving Maive, and Cara, a clear view of the hometown hero—and the blonde bimbo hanging on his arm.

Dressed the part of a casual grand marshal, Finn was typically gorgeous in black tailored trousers and a crisp, white dress shirt. The twenty-something stunner at his side was poured into a slinky, bright red jumpsuit, held up by two miniscule straps. The plunging neckline reached her navel.

Cara wanted to hate her, simply on principle, but as she eyed the blonde, her breaking heart was soothed somewhat, and she snorted with self-satisfaction. Her own outrageous body would fill out that slinky getup far more interestingly than the model thin bimbo.

Besides, Finn was the one Cara hated.

Tempted to slink to the side of the booth, and be as invisible as possible, she remained where she was, in plain view. He knew she'd be here somewhere today, and he wanted her to see this. She would damn well stay.

He stopped at the edge of the sidewalk with the blonde plastered to his side. His cold blue gaze clashed with Cara's. She lifted her chin and wished with all she was worth for laser-beam-eye superpowers. She'd fry him on the spot!

"Stupid boy," Maive mumbled from her chair.

Cara sent her a sidelong glance, steeling her heart against the angry compassion in the old lady's eyes.

"Who's that you've got there, Finn?"

Cara turned at the shouted question, uttered by none other than Stockwell of the future exclusive. Finn flashed a cocky smile at the man, ignoring Maive when she slapped her hand on the plastic arm of her lawn chair.

"This is Vicky, everyone. Vic, say hello to the folks."

"Hey, y'all." Vicky gave the crowd a megawatt smile and preened, pressing her nearly bare bosom against Finn's chest. Cameras clicked and flashed.

"Where are you from, Vicky? How long have you known Finn? What do you do for a living?"

The questions came fast and furious. Jill pushed through the crowd, frantically making her way toward the couple in an attempt to gain control of a circus gone wild.

"Boy!"

Finn ignored Maive's shouted demand, and Vicky didn't have the chance to answer the press as Jill arrived at the center ring. "Everyone, Finn has a prepared statement about our celebration today and if you'd…"

"Hell, Jill." The smile Finn turned on Jill was no more than a bearing of his teeth. "These folks don't want to hear any stuffy speeches. They already know the important points anyway. They're here for the good stuff, and the only way they're going to get it, is by asking questions." He faced the mob. "Next question?"

"Michael Joseph Finnegan!" Maive slammed her gnarled hand on the table. Cara jumped, scrambling to save the large floral arrangement it held. The glass vase bounced and rolled off the edge to shatter on the cement sidewalk at Jill's feet. The raucous crowd was suddenly well behaved. "Have you lost your mind, boy?"

Finn finally looked at Maive. His cocky grin slipped a bit. "Just giving the people what they want, Auntie Maive."

She glared at him, eyeing the blonde plastered to his side. She jerked her head in Cara's direction. "And what about this one?"

Finn's gaze swept to Cara and she fought the heat rising on her cheeks when all eyes swung her way.

"I already *gave* her what she wanted."

****

Finn had to hand it to Cara, she barely flinched, but the quick flash of hurt in her eyes was unmistakable. Bile rose in his throat. Swallowing against the burn, he reminded himself this charade would be over in a few minutes, if Maive would just butt out.

She didn't. She pushed out of her chair, her eyes blazing across the distance. "For the first time in your life, boy, I'm ashamed of you."

187

"Maive." Cara's voice was soft, but firm and when she glanced his way, anger sparked in her green eyes. "He's right. He gave me exactly what I wanted." She reached beneath the table, and then skirted around it, pulling something from her purse. When she stopped in front of him, Vicky tucked closer to his side. Cara didn't even glance at the other woman. Her smile was cold, her eyes frosty as she slapped the check for the renovation against his chest. "For services rendered, stud."

Excited murmurs rippled through the crowd as cameras clicked furiously.

With a final, disdainful sniff, Cara spun away from him, and plowed into a mountain of a man whose dress shirt buttons strained against the girth of his impressive gut. As Finn watched, the man's beefy hands shot out to steady her, grasping her shoulders.

"Cara Cups!" His booming voice held astonishment. "Well, I'll be damned. When did you come back to Palmerton?"

Revulsion darkened her eyes. "Let me go, Timmy." She stumbled backward, wrenching her shoulders free.

Finn flung off Vicky's clinging hands. A low growl escaped his throat as his fist connected with Timmy Faulkner's cheek. Timmy staggered back, but he was a big man. He didn't fall. While the cameras continued to click, Finn took a menacing step forward.

"Keep your hands off her, you bastard."

He met the big man's belligerent glare, and hoped the giant would give him the excuse to throw another punch. A moment later, a punch *was* thrown, but not by Timmy—or Finn. A solid thump to Finn's shoulder had him spinning around to meet Cara's furious gaze. Her hand remained balled into a fist.

"What the hell did you do that for?" he roared.

"I didn't ask for your help!"

His jaw dropped, and the cameras clicked some more.

"Finnie." Vicky whined behind him.

Cara smirked at the blonde's high pitched complaint. Sickening sweetness dripped from her voice as she purred, "I think Vic wants you, Finnie."

"Not now, Vicky!" Finn's voice boomed. Without taking his eyes from Cara, he jerked his thumb in Timmy's direction. "He's the asshole from graduation night!"

All the crap he threw at her today hadn't rattled her composure, but the mention of that night had shadows flitting across her expressive face. She paled, and his heart squeezed in his chest.

"Cara." He held out his hand, his appeal sounding tortured to his own ears. Timmy, who had apparently been enjoying the show up until now, took exception to the asshole remark, and drew back his fist. Cara pivoted, snapping her elbow. The crowd gave a collective groan at the sound of bone meeting cartilage, with bone winning.

"Out of my way." The sudden silence was broken by the arrival of Tom O'Shea, resembling a thundercloud searching for somewhere to unload. The crowd gave him a wide birth as he pushed through the throng of avid onlookers with Hannah close on his heels.

The press corps erupted in a frenzy of fascination, their cameras aimed and clicking at the three furious, towering males. One with a Super Bowl ring, one searching for somewhere to plant the side of beef that passed for his hand, and the last bleeding to beat the band. All of whom were frowning at the Amazon with the mean left hook.

"Is there a problem here, Cara?" Tom spoke over Timmy's pained curses.

"No, Daddy." Tears welled in her eyes and she dragged her gaze from Finn's. "I just had some unfinished business to take care of."

Hannah slipped her arm around Cara's waist. Tom wrapped an arm around the both of them. They walked away to the sound of Maive's cackling laughter.

Chapter Twenty-Four

Meggy sprawled back in an overstuffed chair. She tipped the wine glass to her lips. "I have to say, that was one *hell* of an incorporation celebration."

The room erupted in laughter.

Exhausted from the stress of the day, Cara couldn't think of anywhere else she'd rather be. Daddy and Ryan had carried her new furniture in from the storage area and set it up in her studio when Mary insisted Maive, who arrived not long after they had left the celebration, shouldn't have to climb the stairs to Cara's apartment to find a seat.

Hannah and Erin called for pizza. Meggy and Shan showed up with several bottles of wine.

Her family closed ranks around her after the disaster in front of the press tent. Several friends stopped by to give them circus updates, throughout the afternoon.

Needless to say, the celebration bombed. After Finn's outrageous performance, the press wasn't interested in anything to do with the town. They wanted the good stuff he'd mentioned. They hounded Vicky, the underwear model, who stomped off in a tizzy when Finn left her high and dry to race off in the convertible he'd been scheduled to ride in for the parade.

The press camped outside Cara's studio for a

while, until Tom went out and had a little chat with them. They promptly decided to go after easier prey. A bleeding Timmy Faulkner hadn't been seen again, after shouting *no comment*, before jumping into his brother's pick-up. Apparently having his nose broken by a woman was more than his colossal ego could take, especially since there were pictures documenting their altercation this time.

Cara hoped he didn't sue.

Jill did what she could to salvage the day. The parade marched on, sans one grand marshal, but the high school band was wonderful, or so everyone said. They hadn't raised the kind of money Jill hoped for. However, the townspeople contributed more than expected. There was nothing like a good nose breaking to keep people milling about and gossiping, while buying beer and soda at extravagant prices.

Shan and Mary eventually left to check on Shan's boys, and Tom and Hannah followed not long after them. Though Cara would never be as close to Daddy as she'd been as a little girl, she found she could forgive him, and had. And Hannah? Well, as Meggy said, she seemed nice.

"Are you going to talk to him?" Maive studied Cara as she waited for Ryan and Erin to bring the car around to take her home.

Cara sighed and shot Meggy a glance where she was cleaning the mess from the pizza. Cara knew this was coming. As cantankerous as Maive was, she was a romantic at heart, and she loved her grandnephew. It was only a matter of time before she'd have her heart broken, just like Cara.

"He doesn't have anything to say to me, Maive. He

made that pretty clear, don't you think?"

"What he made clear is what a total ass he can be sometimes."

"You'll get no argument from me on that point."

"He has plenty to say to you, girl, and that's the problem."

Cara sighed. She was too tired for riddles tonight. "What's that supposed to mean, Maive?"

Maive patted her cheek. "Call me after you talk to him, so I can crow a little."

Cara stared after her as she left. She didn't know what was wrong with everyone. Why was she the only one who understood what Finn had tried so hard to say with his outrageous performance this afternoon? She heard his message loud and clear. "Don't love me, Cara. I can't love you back. This is who and what I am."

He was wrong, of course. He was so much more than a playboy ex-athlete, but unless or until he saw that himself, nothing would change. In the meantime, she wasn't going to continue to let her heart be battered by the knowledge he didn't love her. She had her work, she had her family and friends, and she'd had four glorious weeks with the man she'd loved her whole life.

It was time she moved beyond her lifelong fascination with Michael Finnegan.

****

Finn banged his shin on something hard and bulky. He hissed a vicious curse. The studio was pitch-black, but he didn't dare turn on a light.

He ran his fingers over the unexpected obstruction. Buttery soft leather met his touch. Hell, she moved furniture in already? Didn't she know the floor needed a few days to cure?

Thankfully, the stairs were new and didn't squeak. He climbed to the second floor apartment, quietly unlocking the door. He stepped lightly, not wanting any tell-tale creaks to alert her to his presence until he could slip into the bedroom. Once he had her in his arms, he figured he could romance her into listening to him, and forgiving him.

If that didn't work, he'd beg.

He struggled against the urge to race through the apartment, laughing like an ass. Cara loved him! If what Evan Malone told him was true, she had for years. The knowledge rattled him, even as it thrilled and humbled him.

The last person he expected when he opened the door to the penthouse an hour ago had been her art dealer. The big man pushed his way through the door and demanded to know what Finn's intentions were toward Cara.

Finn hadn't been thrilled to learn his instincts about the man were right on the mark, but the rest of what he learned more than made up for the burn of jealousy while listening to the man's frank comments.

According to Malone, she'd been in love with Finn for years, at least eight, and probably longer than that. She hadn't lost interest after a couple of years, or once his football career ended, deciding there must be something or someone better out there. That kind of love was lasting. Love that deep would weather life's storms and come out stronger on the other side.

His charmed life had been restored.

Malone had no reason to lie about Cara's long-term feelings for Finn, just the opposite, in fact. The man was in love with Cara, had been for years. Her art dealer enjoyed making it clear that if she was finally over Finn, after what he'd done at the anniversary celebration today, Evan would do whatever was necessary to win her once and for all, and keep her.

And if by some miracle, she was still in love with Finn, Evan gave notice that Finn had better never hurt her again or he'd have Evan Malone to deal with. Finn wasn't about to let any other man have her. He'd spend the rest of his life doing everything in his power to make her happy.

The light above the stove cast a faint glow over the tiny kitchen and living area, saving his shins from further damage as he kicked off his shoes. He pulled the shirt over his head, and unsnapped his jeans, dropping them and his briefs on the couch. Naked, he tiptoed to the bedroom door, cringing as he slowly swung it open.

Approaching the bed, he could just make out the bump she made beneath the sheet. He smiled at the sight of her head buried beneath the cool cotton.

He tried not to jostle the bed, sliding in beside her, but wasn't completely successful. She grumbled a protest at being disturbed. He leaned over her, crooning. "Shhh. It's okay, baby. It's just me."

The bed jostled then, though neither of them moved. He blinked when the room suddenly flooded with light.

On the other side of the bed, Cara gasped and stared, her arm still outstretched toward the lamp. Finn's eyes widened in horrified surprise, and he glanced down at the bump lying under him, still buried beneath the sheet. A slender hand emerged, shoving the sheet down to reveal the blonde head and scowling face of Meggy Calhoun.

"Jesus!" Finn scrambled out of the bed as though it were on fire.

Meggy scooted up against the headboard with a huff, and took her time eyeing his naked body as he searched for something to cover himself. He snatched Cara's robe from the foot of the bed, turning around to shove his arms in the sleeves. They came to just below his elbows, and the garment ended far above his knees.

****

Cara sat up, pushing her tangled hair from her face. Though her frilly, yellow robe wasn't as funny on Finn as it should be, she had the stray wish that one of those pushy press people from this morning would magically appear with their camera right about now.

"What the hell are you doing here?" He glared at Meggy as he knotted the sash at his waist.

"Funny, but I was about to ask you the same question." She turned to Cara. "You were right about his body. He looks great naked. Too bad he's such an incredible asshole."

"Meggy." Cara sighed.

"Don't Meggy me. You aren't going to listen to his pathetic excuses are you? What he did was rotten." Meggy eyed his muscular form in the silky yellow confection. Crossing her arms, she glanced dismissively from the top of his head to his bare feet. "If I was a foot taller and a hundred pounds heavier, I'd kick his ass."

Finn returned Meggy's glare for several heartbeats, but when he turned to Cara, his blue eyes softened.

"We need to talk, baby."

Cara stiffened. How dare he look so sincere? "That's not necessary. You made yourself perfectly clear this morning."

"Atta girl!" Meggy crowed. "Don't let those incredible pecs scramble your brains."

"Shut up, Meggy," Finn growled.

Meggy sat up in the bed and pointed a finger at him. "Don't you tell me to shut up. You're not the boss of me!"

He stalked to the foot of the bed. Bending at the waist, he slapped both hands on the mattress and leaned over Meggy. His powerful arms bracketed her legs beneath the sheet. She tucked them under her, out of his reach.

"I'm giving you two minutes to get dressed and get out of here. If you're still here after that, I'm hauling you downstairs in your jammies and dumping your ass on the sidewalk."

Meggy was silent for a moment, and her eyes shot to Cara, who sighed and tossed the covers aside to climb from the bed. She walked to the closet and pulled out another robe.

Meggy frowned. "You can't kick me out of here. This is Cara's place, not yours."

Finn straightened. The shoulder seams of the robe strained when he crossed his arms over those impressive pecs. "A minute, thirty."

Slamming the covers aside, Meggy slipped from the bed and snatched her clothes from a chair. "I never realized what a jerk you are."

Finn ignored the insult, now that Meggy was following his directive.

She shoved slender legs into her jeans, whipping them up under her mid-thigh sleep shirt. "You know, Finn. She's never done anything but love you."

"Meggy." Cara shook her head.

Shooting her an apologetic grimace, Meggy scooped up her purse and blouse and stomped across the room to stop in front of him. Despite the top of her head only coming to his collarbone, she lifted a belligerent chin and poked him in the center of his chest with her index finger.

"You'd better not hurt her anymore."

His big hand closed around her finger and held her there. "I won't hurt her, Meggy. I promise." He raised her hand and flipped it over to place a kiss on her palm.

"Geez." Rolling her eyes, she tugged her hand free. She tossed Cara a pitying glance over one shoulder while walking to the door. "Good luck, girlfriend."

"I see what you mean about her being your bodyguard," he said after the apartment door clicked shut.

Cara sighed and sat on the edge of the bed. "What do you want, Finn?"

He sat beside her. "I want *you*."

She stiffened. "You wanted Vic this morning. I don't think you know *what* you want."

"Aw, baby. I'm sorry." He picked up a lock of her hair and rubbed it between his finger and thumb. "That was pretty shitty of me. I was an asshole."

She tugged her hair free and stood. "Yes, you are." She left him sitting on the bed and went into the kitchen. She was grabbing a bottle of water from the fridge when he filled the doorway.

"I panicked, Cara."

She leaned her hip against the counter. "You panicked?"

He nodded, but stayed where he was. "Things

between us were moving so fast. One day you were here and I was spending all this time in your studio, and the next you were sleeping in my bed and…"

"Hold it right there, buster." She aimed the water bottle at him. "I didn't want to hire you in the first place, remember? That was your idea. And I distinctly recall you offering your bed while the studio was ripped up. That was your idea, too."

"I'm not saying it's your fault."

"You'd damned well better not be!"

Tired and heartsick, she didn't want to fight with him. All she wanted was to be left alone. With a sigh, she sank onto a kitchen chair. "Just say whatever it is you want to say and go."

His eyes wary, he crossed the room and lowered to the chair on her right. She didn't flinch or pull away when he took one of her hands in his. Instead, she stared down at their entwined hands, his large and wide palmed, hers delicate with long, tapered artist's fingers. He played with them.

"When I took that hit to the knee," he began, "something died in me. I'm a ball player. My whole life, football was always there. When my parents died, when I moved away from home for the first time. Then, all of a sudden, the sport I love was gone. The one constant in my life was ripped away from me, and I spiraled. When Andrea left, I went a little wild. I figured the whole world was looking at me and thinking, poor schmuck, can't play ball, can't keep his wife. I started dating women just to prove to the world I was still man enough to land a beautiful woman, even if I couldn't play ball anymore. Every time my picture showed up on one of those rags with a different woman on my arm, it was like a full color announcement that Andrea was the failure, instead of me.

"But after a while, I realized I was choosing women I could easily walk away from, before they walked away from me. I did the same with work. I avoided anything important, anything permanent. I turned down all offers for permanent work, preferring guest spots and limited contracts to the possibility of something fulfilling that could disappear on the whims of fate. Just like football. Just like Andrea. Just like my mother."

"You rebuilt the Sawyer House, Finn, that's permanent. And you built the boys' camp. That's important." He quickly glanced up from their hands, as if surprised. "Doc told me about the camp."

He disregarded her comment with a shake of his head. "I just set it up. Doc runs it. I spend a couple of weeks with the kids and move on to a new bunch the next summer."

Her brow wrinkled in confusion. "What does any of this have to do with me? I didn't make any demands of you, and yet you acted out that little scene today like I was some kind of fatal attraction. All you had to say was *it's over*. I would have accepted that. You should have just told me you wanted to move on, instead of embarrassing me in front of the entire town with Vicky."

"Oh, baby. I'm sorry about Vicky. Like I said, I panicked, and it seemed kinder to hurt you now, rather than later after things got even more complicated."

"Kinder?" Yanking her hand from his, she jumped to her feet. "I think I've heard enough. What do you want, Finn? Do you want me to accept your apology?

Fine, I accept. Now, go!"

He stood as well. "I didn't come just to apologize. I came because I'm in love with you. Because I screwed up, and I don't want to lose you."

She crossed her arms and gave him a falsely patient stare. "You're in love with me. Okay. So? What? You've decided now that you don't mind hurting me later?"

"Damn it, Cara, I know I'm making a mess of this, but I do love you, and I won't hurt you. I give you my word." He brushed her cheek with his fingertip. She turned her head aside, avoiding his touch.

"What's changed since this morning?" She shook her head and sighed. "I can't spend the next six months waiting for you to show up with Sissy or Buffy, parading some woman in front of me because you think it will be kinder to hurt me then, rather than in a year. I received your message, loud and clear. Let's just leave it at that."

He ignored the reference to other women, dipping his head to gaze straight in her eyes. "This morning I hadn't spoken to Evan Malone."

She blinked. "Evan?" Of all things he could have said, she never expected that. "Why would you talk to Evan?"

"Because he showed up at my penthouse."

"Why?"

He met her bewildered gaze. "Because he's in love with you."

She gave a startled laugh. "No, he isn't." Finn said nothing, simply waited. "He's just a friend."

"Tell me there isn't a history there, Cara. Tell me he isn't the *one*."

Her mind supplied the memory of them standing beside her bed. *Have you ever been with a man, baby? I...yes, once.* His somber blue gaze bore into hers. Guilt flooded her and she glanced away.

He moved a step closer, his deep voice husky with emotion. "I don't care who you've been with before me, Cara. God knows I don't have room to talk. What I care about is what you feel for him. What he feels for you."

She stared into his eyes and the emotion she read there brought a sting of tears to her own. "He's my friend."

He nodded and brushed away the single tear that escaped with his finger. "He's your friend, and he's in love with you."

She shook her head in denial.

"A man in love can spot another man in love," he murmured, his gaze running over her face before returning to her eyes. "Particularly when they're both in love with the same woman."

"Finn." She whimpered when he continued to stroke her cheek with the tip of his finger.

"He told me you were in love with another man when he met you. That you've been in love with this man for years. Am I that man, Cara?"

She began to cry in earnest at having her yearning heart laid bare. Speaking was impossible. She nodded.

He bowed his head until his forehead rested against hers. "I'm in love with you, Cara. I've been afraid to take a chance on anything that matters for so long. Afraid it wouldn't last. When I saw you with Evan yesterday, I was pissed off enough to decide it was time to let you go." His head lifted, and he cupped her chin with his hand. "But I can't. I need you, Cara. I need to share that love with you. I know it's fast, but when I walked in and found you sitting in Maive's parlor, it was as though I had been sacked by an entire defensive line."

Her eyes drifted shut on a teary laugh. "I know the feeling."

He chuckled, wrapping his arms around her to pull her close. "You've been sacked by a defensive line, have you?"

She opened her eyes, smiling through tears. "No." She shook her head. "For me it was a flock of butterflies." A laugh escaped, seeing the puzzlement on his face. "I was eleven when I got my first glimpse of Finn the Fine in action under a tree near the school gymnasium. You smiled at me and winked. My stomach fluttered as if I had swallowed a flock of butterflies. I've loved you ever since."

His mouth crashed down on hers, but after a moment his head jerked back and he grinned. "You were the little girl spying on Alice Butler and me behind the gym?"

She nodded. "Guilty as charged, but not so little."

He threw back his head and laughed. Scooping her up in his arms, he carried her to the bedroom. "If my former teammates could see me now, an all-pro quarterback in a yellow frilly robe with a sexy bundle in his arms."

She blushed at his compliment, fingering the lapel of the robe. "Forget your teammates. Meggy's the one you have to worry about. She *has* seen you in my frilly yellow robe, and she has a long memory."

He stopped beside her bed, his brows drawing

together in a frown.

"Poor baby." She patted his cheek in sympathy, biting her lip to keep from laughing.

"You know her better than I do. How does she feel about bribes?"

Cara lost the battle with her laughter. His eyes flashed with wicked intent. Holding her out over the mattress, he dropped her. She landed with a shriek in the center of the bed. Finn soon followed to cover her body with his. He dropped a kiss on her nose, and his smile slipped into seriousness.

"I'm sorry I wasn't there for you last night. Evan told me what happened with your father and Hannah."

She swallowed the lump in her throat. "They've been through hell."

"It hasn't been easy for any of you, but at least now you know Tom didn't deliberately set out to hurt anyone. He was caught up in an unbearable situation." She nodded. "Tom loves you, baby. And Hannah is a nice woman."

"I know."

He lowered his mouth to hers, nibbling at the corners of her lips. The familiar flame only Finn could fan warmed her and she melted under his delicious ministrations. She joined him in his nibbling until he pulled back to leer down at her.

Pure deviltry sparkled in his eyes. "Now, about that dirt."

A word about the author...

Raised in the Boston area, Mac and her husband live in Phoenix where they raised two rambunctious little boys into wonderful men. Dirt bikes and ESPN are the order around their house, and life at the "Testosterone Ranch" more closely resembles one of today's wacky reality shows than yesterday's *Leave It To Beaver*.

The grandmother of two, Mac's love of the romance genre has been a lifelong affair. A bout with breast cancer strengthened her resolve to see her stories shared with others. As of today, Mac is a five-year survivor, living her dream.

http://mackenziecrowne.com

Thank you for purchasing
this publication of The Wild Rose Press, Inc.
For other wonderful stories of romance,
please visit our on-line bookstore at
www.thewildrosepress.com.

For questions or more information
contact us at
info@thewildrosepress.com.

The Wild Rose Press, Inc.
www.thewildrosepress.com

To visit with authors of
The Wild Rose Press, Inc.
join our yahoo loop at
http://groups.yahoo.com/group/thewildrosepress/